"Come in." The masculine drawl coming from within was low and gruff.

The back of her neck prickled. If she had to pick a description to pair that voice with, she'd say impatient. Or sexy. Two words you wouldn't want associated with the army psychiatrist charged with your daughter's care.

He's probably fat and bald, Jessi.

Comforted by that thought, she pushed the lever down and opened the door.

He wasn't fat. Or bald.

The man seated behind the military-issue desk had a full head of jet-black hair. Something about his profile tugged at her, just as his voice had.

"I'll be with you in a minute."

Her gaze landed on the nameplate on the doctor's desk.

Jessi froze. Her gaze flicked back to the portion of his face she could see. Recognition roared to life and images of heated kisses in the grass beside the creek flashed through her head.

Clinton Marks. A ghost from her past…a rite of passage.

A moment in time.

And yet here he was, sitting across from her in living color.

Dear Reader,

Sometimes life gives us second chances: a dream job we passed up for something else, a return trip to a childhood home, a first love that was lost many years ago. And sometimes...sometimes we come to understand why things happened the way they did in the past.

Thank you for joining Jessi and Clint as they unexpectedly come face-to-face after years apart. As Jessi struggles to understand what went wrong between them Clint wrestles with the demons that haunt him. And maybe, through the power of forgiveness and with an approving nod from fate, they can rediscover a love they thought long dead.

Clint and Jessi's journey has a special place in my heart. I hope you enjoy reading their story as much as I loved writing it!

Much love

Tina Beckett

THE SOLDIER
SHE COULD
NEVER FORGET

BY
TINA BECKETT

First published in Great Britain 2015
by Mills & Boon, an imprint of Harlequin (UK) Limited,
Eton House, 18-24 Paradise Road, Richmond, Surrey, TW9 1SR

© 2015 Tina Beckett

ISBN: 978-0-263-25782-3

(Harlequin (UK) Limited's policy is to use papers that are natural,
renewable and recyclable products and made from wood grown in
sustainable forests. The logging and manufacturing processes conform
to the legal environmental regulations of the country of origin.

Born to a family that was always on the move, **Tina Beckett** learned to pack a suitcase almost before she knew how to tie her shoes. Fortunately she met a man who also loved to travel, and she snapped him right up. Married for over twenty years, Tina has three wonderful children and has lived in gorgeous places such as Portugal and Brazil.

Living where English reading material is difficult to find has its drawbacks, however. Tina had to come up with creative ways to satisfy her love for romance novels, so she picked up her pen and tried writing one. After her tenth book she realised she was hooked. She was officially a writer.

A three-time Golden Heart finalist, and fluent in Portuguese, Tina now divides her time between the United States and Brazil. She loves to use exotic locales as the backdrop for many of her stories. When she's not writing you can find her either on horseback or soldering stained glass panels for her home.

Tina loves to hear from readers. You can contact her through her website or 'friend' her on Facebook.

Books by Tina Beckett

Visit the author profile page at millsandboon.co.uk for more titles

To my children. You bring me joy, every single day.

Praise for Tina Beckett

'…a tension-filled emotional story with just the right amount of drama. The author's vivid description of the Brazilian jungle and its people make this story something special.'

—*RT Book Reviews* on
Doctor's Guide to Dating in the Jungle

'Medical Romance lovers will definitely like *NYC Angels: Flirting with Danger* by Tina Beckett—for who *doesn't* like a good forbidden romance?'

—*HarlequinJunkie* on
NYC Angels: Flirting with Danger

PROLOGUE

Twenty-two years earlier

"JESS. DON'T CRY."

The low words came from behind her, the slight rasp to his tone giving away his identity immediately.

Jessi stiffened, but she didn't turn around. Oh, God. He'd followed her. She hadn't realized anyone had even seen her tearful flight out of the auditorium, much less come after her. But they had. And those low gravely tones didn't belong to Larry Riley, who'd had a crush on her for ages, or her father—*thank God!*—but Clinton Marks, the last person she would have expected to care about what she thought or felt.

"I—I'm not."

One scuffed motorcycle boot appeared on the other side of the log where she was seated, the footwear in stark contrast to the flowing green graduation gowns they both wore—and probably topping the school's list of banned attire for tonight's ceremony.

The gown made her smile. Clint, in what amounted to a dress. She hoped someone had gotten a picture of that.

He sat beside her as she hurried to scrub away the evidence of her anguish. Not soon enough, though, because cool fingers touched her chin, turning her head toward him. "You're a terrible liar, Jessi May."

Somehow hearing the pet name spoken in something other than his normal mocking tones caused hot tears to wash back into her eyes and spill over, trailing down her cheeks until one of them reached his thumb. He brushed it away, his touch light.

She'd never seen him like this. Maybe the reality of the night had struck him, as well. In a few short hours, her group of friends would all be flying off to start new lives. Larry and Clint would be headed for boot camp. And her best friend would be spending the next year in Spain on a college exchange program.

They were all leaving.

All except Jessi.

She was stuck here in Richmond—with an overly strict father who'd come down hard when he'd heard Larry was gearing up for a career in the army. The papers weren't signed yet, but they would be in a matter of days. She'd done her best to hide the news, but her dad had been bound to find out sooner or later. He didn't want her involved with a military man. Kind of unreasonable in a place where those kinds of men were a dime a dozen.

Maybe she should have picked an out-of-state college, rather than choosing to commute from home. But as an only child, she hadn't quite been able to bring herself to leave her mom alone in that huge house.

"What's going on, Jess?" Clint's voice came back to her, pulling her from her pity party.

She shrugged. "My dad, he… He just…" It sounded so stupid to complain about her father to someone who flouted authority every chance he got. If only she could be like that. But she'd always been a people pleaser. The trait had gotten worse once she'd been old enough to realize her mom's "vitamins" were actually antidepressants.

Instead of the flip attitude she'd expected from Clint, though, his eyes turned this cold shade of gunmetal gray that made her shiver. His fingers tightened slightly on her chin. "Your father what, Jess? What did he do?"

Her teeth came down on her lip when she realized what he was saying. There'd been rumors about Clint's family, that his father was the reason he was the way he was.

Her dad was nothing like that.

"He didn't do anything. He's just…unreasonable. He's against me being with people like you or Larry."

His head tilted. "Me…and Larry." His mouth turned up at the corners. "I see your dad's point. Larry and I are definitely cut from the same cloth."

They weren't. Not at all. Larry was like her. He was all about good grades and toeing the line. Clint, however, lived on the edge of trouble—his skull tattoo and pierced ear making teachers shake their heads, while all the girls swooned.

Including her.

His words made her smile, though. "You're both going into the army."

"Ah, I see. Your father wouldn't like me, though, in or out of the army."

Her smile widened. "He's protective."

He made a sound low in his throat that might have been a laugh. "The thing is…" his eyes found hers again and a warm hand cupped the back of her neck "…I didn't know I was even in the running. So I'm neck and neck with Larry *straight-A* Riley."

Something hot flared low in her belly. Clint had never, ever given the slightest hint he was interested in her. And yet here he was. Beside her. The only person to notice her walk off the stage and slip out the door after getting her diploma. The only one who'd followed her.

"I—I… Did you want to be?"

"No."

The word should have cut her to the quick, except the low pained tone was somehow at odds with his denial.

"Clint…?" Her fingertips moved to his cheek, her eyes meeting his with something akin to desperation.

Another sound rumbled up from his chest, coming out as a groan this time. Then, something she'd never dreamed possible—in all of her eighteen years—happened.

Clinton Marks—bad boy extraordinaire—whispered her name. Right before his mouth came down and covered hers.

CHAPTER ONE

"CHELSEA'S NEW DOCTOR arrived today." The nurse's matter-of-fact words stopped her in her tracks.

Jessica Marie Riley blinked and turned back to the main desk of the Richmond VA hospital, where her twenty-one-year-old daughter had spent the past two months of her life—a frail shell of the robust soldier who'd been so proud of toughing it out at army boot camp.

It had always been just her and Chelsea against the world. They'd supported each other, laughed together, told each other everything.

Until she'd returned from her very first tour of duty as a former POW...and a different person.

"He did?" Jessi's stomach lurched. Her daughter's last doctor had left unexpectedly and she'd been told there was a possibility she'd be shuffled between the other military psychiatrists until a replacement could be found.

Maria, the nurse who'd admitted Chelsea and had shown a huge amount of compassion toward both of them, hesitated. She knew what a sore spot this was. "Dr. Cordoba had some family issues and resigned his commission. It really wasn't his fault."

Jessi knew from experience how devastating some family issues could be. But with the hurricane that had just gouged its way up the coast, her work schedule at Scott's

Memorial had been brutal. The shortage of ER doctors had never been more evident, and it had driven the medical staff to the brink of exhaustion. It also made her a little short on patience.

And now her daughter had lost the only doctor she'd seemed to bond with during her hospitalization.

Jess had hoped they'd finally get some answers about why Chelsea had spiraled into the depths of despair after coming home—and that she'd finally find a way to be at peace with whatever had happened in that squalid prison camp.

That tiny thread of hope had now been chopped in two. Anger flared at how easy it was for people like Dr. Cordoba to leave patients who counted on him.

Not fair, Jess. You're not walking in his shoes.

But the man wasn't walking in hers, either. He hadn't been there on that terrible day when her daughter had tried to take her own life.

She couldn't imagine how draining it was to deal with patients displaying symptoms of post-traumatic stress disorder on a daily basis, but Jessi had been handed some pretty awful cases herself. No one saw her throwing in the towel and moving on to some cushy private gig.

Maria came around the desk and touched her arm. "Her new doctor is one of the top in his field. He's dedicated his life to treating patients like your daughter—in fact, he transferred from California just to take over Dr. Cordoba's PTSD patients. At least until we can get a permanent replacement. He's already been to see Chelsea and reviewed her chart."

Top in his field. That had to be good, right? But if he was only temporary…

"What did he think?"

This time, the nurse wouldn't quite meet her eyes. "I'm

not sure. He asked me to send you to his office as soon as you arrived. He's down the hall, first door on your left."

Dr. Cordoba's old office.

The thread of anger continued to wind through her veins, despite Maria's encouraging words. This was Chelsea's third doctor. That averaged out to more than one a month. How long did this newest guy plan on sticking around?

A sudden thought came to her. "How did the hospital find this doctor so quickly?"

"This is what he does. He rotates between military hospitals, filling in..." The sound of yelling came from down the hallway, stopping Maria's explanation in its tracks. A woman headed their way, pushing a wheelchair, while the older gentleman in the seat bellowed something unintelligible, his fist shaking in the air.

"Excuse me," said the nurse, quickly moving toward the pair. She threw over her shoulder, "Chelsea's doctor is in his office. He's expecting you. Just go on in." Her attention shifted toward the agitated patient. "Mr. Ballenger, what's wrong?"

Not wanting to stand there like a gawker, Jessi stiffened her shoulders and headed in the direction Maria had indicated.

First door on the left.

All she wanted to do was skip the requisite chit-chat and go straight to Chelsea's room. But that was evidently not going to happen. Not until she met with the newest member of Chelsea's treatment team.

Feeling helpless and out of control was rapidly becoming the norm for Jessi. And she didn't like it. At all.

She stopped in front of the door and glared at the nameplate. Dr. Cordoba's credentials were still prominently displayed in the cheap gold-colored frame. The new guy really was new.

Damn, and she'd forgotten to ask the nurse his name. It didn't really matter. He'd introduce himself. So would she, and then he'd ask her how she was. That's what they always did.

Tell the truth? Or nod and say, "Fine," just like she did every other time someone asked her?

She lifted her hand and rapped on the solid wood door.

"Come in." The masculine drawl coming from within was low and gruff.

The back of her neck prickled, the sensation sweeping across her shoulders and down her arms, lifting every fine hair in its path. If she had to pick a description to pair that voice with, she'd say impatient. Or sexy. Two words you didn't want associated with an army psychiatrist. Or any psychiatrist, for that matter. And certainly not one charged with her daughter's care.

He's probably fat and bald, Jess.

Comforted by that thought, she pushed the lever down and opened the door.

He wasn't fat. Or bald.

His head was turned to the side, obscuring most of his face, but the man seated behind the gray, military-issue desk had a full head of jet-black hair, the sides short in typical army fashion, while the longer top fell casually across his forehead. Jessi spied a few strands of gray woven through the hair at his temple.

He appeared to be intently studying his computer screen. Something about his profile tugged at her, just like his voice had. She shook off the sensation, rubbing her upper arms as she continued to stand there.

He had to be pushing forty, judging from the lines beside his eyes as well as the long crease down the side of his left cheek. The result of a dimple utilized far too many times?

Something in her mind swirled back to life as if some

hazy image was trying to imprint itself on her consciousness.

"Feel free to sit," he said. "I'll be with you in a minute."

She swallowed, all thoughts of new doctors and balding men fading as worry nibbled at the pit of her stomach. Was something wrong with Chelsea? She tried to open her mouth to ask, but the words were suddenly stuck in her throat. Maybe that's why Maria wouldn't quite meet her eyes. Had Chelsea made another suicide attempt? Surely the nurse would have said something had that been the case.

Pulling one of the two chairs back a few inches, she eased into it, her gaze shuffling around the room, trying to find anything that would calm her nerves.

What it landed on was the nameplate on the doctor's desk. Not Dr. Cordoba's. Instead...

Jessi froze. She blinked rapidly to clear her vision and focused on the letters again, sliding across each one individually and hoping that an *a* would somehow morph into an *e*.

Her gaze flicked back to the portion of his face she could see. Recognition roared to life this time.

She should have realized that prickling sensation hadn't been a fluke when she'd heard his voice. But she would never have dreamed...

Images of heated kisses and stolen moments in the grass beside the creek near her high school flashed through her head.

God. Clinton Marks. A ghost from her past...a rite of passage.

That's all it had been. A moment in time. And yet here he was, sitting across from her in living color.

Worse, he was evidently her daughter's new doctor. How was that possible?

Maybe he wouldn't recognize her.

When his gray eyes finally swung her way, that hope dropped like a boulder from a cliff. A momentary burst of shock crossed his face, jaw squaring, lips tightening. Then the familiar mocking smile from school appeared, and his gaze dropped to her empty ring finger.

"I should have recognized his last name," he said. "Me and Larry. Neck and neck…"

His murmured words turned their shared past into a silly nursery rhyme. His next words shattered that illusion, however. "Still married to him?"

She swallowed. "Widowed."

Larry had died in a car accident a few months after their wedding. Right after he'd discovered from a mutual friend that she'd been seen returning to the auditorium with Clint the night of graduation. He'd asked her a question she'd refused to answer, and then he'd roared off into the night, never to come home.

"I'm sorry."

Was he? She couldn't tell by looking at him. The Clinton Marks of twenty-two years ago had worn this exact same mask during high school, not letting any kind of real emotion seep through. The earring was gone, and his tattoo was evidently hidden beneath the long sleeves of his shirt, but he still projected an attitude of blasé amusement. She'd seen that mask crack one time. And that memory now kept her glued to her chair instead of storming out and demanding that the "punk" who'd slept with her and then left without a word be removed from her daughter's case immediately and replaced with someone who actually cared.

Someone who had at least a modicum of empathy.

He did.

She'd seen it.

Experienced it.

Had felt gentle fingers tunnel through her hair, palms cupping her face and blotting her tears.

She sucked down a deep breath, realizing he was waiting for a response. "Thank you. He's been gone a long time."

And so have you. She kept that to herself, however.

His gaze shifted back to something on his monitor before fastening on her face once again. "Your daughter. There's no chance that…?"

"I'm sorry?" Her sluggish brain tried to sift through his words, but right now it seemed to be misfiring.

"Chelsea. Her chart says she's twenty-one."

It clicked. What he was saying. The same question Larry had asked her before storming off: *Is the kid even mine?* Pain slashed through her all over again. "She's my husband's."

His jaw hardened further. "You didn't waste much time marrying him after I left."

She was sure it would have seemed that way to him. But Clint had been already on his way out of town. Gone long before he'd actually left. There had never been any question of him staying, and he'd used protection that night, so surely he knew Chelsea couldn't be his. But, then, condoms had been known to fail.

"You weren't coming back. You said so yourself." The fact that there was a hint of accusation in her voice didn't seem to faze him.

"No. I wasn't."

And there you had it. Clinton Marks was the same old looking-out-for-number-one boy she remembered. Only now he was packed into a man's body.

A hard, masculine body with a face capable of breaking a million hearts.

He'd broken at least one.

Only she hadn't admitted it at the time. Instead, she'd

moved on with her life the day he'd left, doing everything in her power to erase the memory of that devastating night. She'd thought she'd succeeded with Larry. And she *had* loved him, in her own way. He'd been everything Clint hadn't. Kind. Dependable. Permanent.

And willing to give up his career to be with her.

Three months later they'd married, and she'd become pregnant.

And Jessi certainly loved the child she'd made with him.

In fact, that was why she was here: Chelsea.

"It was a long time ago..." Her gaze flicked to the nameplate, and she made a quick decision about how to treat this unexpected meeting. And how to address him. "Dr. Marks, if you think that what happened between two kids—and that's all we were—will hinder your ability to help my daughter—"

"Are we really going to do this, Jessi May?" His brow cocked as the name slid effortlessly past his lips. "Pretend that night never happened? I'm interested in treating Chelsea, not in making a play for you, if that's what you're worried about."

Her face heated. "Of course I'm not."

And he was making it perfectly clear that he had no more interest in her now than he had all those years ago.

"I only asked about her parentage because I would need to remove myself from her case if it turned out she was... not Larry's."

In other words, if Chelsea were his.

What a relief it must be to him that she wasn't.

What a mess. Not quite a love triangle, but almost. There was one side missing, though. Larry had been infatuated with her. She'd been infatuated with Clint. And Clint had loved no one but himself.

Which brought her back to her current dilemma. "My daughter is sensitive. If she thinks you're treating her to work your way up some military ladder, you could damage her even more."

"I'm very good at what I do. And I'm not interested in going any further up the ladder."

The words weren't said with pride. In fact, there was an edge of strain behind them.

She believed him. The word *Colonel* in front of his name attested to decades of hard work. She knew from her father's days in the army that it took around twenty years to make that particular rank. Her dad had made it all the way up to general before his death five years ago.

In fact, her father was why she and Clint had wound up by the creek. When he'd realized Larry was headed for a military career her dad had gone off on her, using her mom's depression as ammunition for his position. The night of graduation had brought home all the changes that had been about to happen. Everyone she cared about had been on their way out of her life.

Only Larry had changed his mind at the last minute, inexplicably deciding to study at a local community college and take classes in agriculture instead.

Her glance went back to Clint, whose jaw still bore a hard edge of tension.

Me and Larry...neck and neck.

And Larry had stayed behind. With her.

The only one who knew about her dad besides her girlfriends was... "Oh, my God. You told him, didn't you? You told Larry about my father."

He didn't deny it. He didn't even blink. "How is he? Your father?"

"He's gone. He died five years ago." The pain in her chest grew. They may never have seen eye to eye about a lot of things, but she'd loved the man. And in spite of his shortcomings, he'd been a tower of strength after Larry had died and she'd been left alone, pregnant and grieving.

"I'm sorry." Clint reached across the desk to cover her hand with his. "Your mom?"

"She's okay. Worried about Chelsea. Just like I am."

He pulled back and nodded. "Let's discuss your daughter, then."

"The nurse said you've already seen her, and you've read her chart, so you know what she tried to do."

"Let's talk about that, and then we'll see her together." He pulled a yellow legal pad from a drawer of his desk and laid it in front of him. He was neat, she'd give him that, and it surprised her. Around ten pencils, all sharpened to fine points, were lined up side by side, and a single good-quality pen was at the end of the row. Nothing else adorned the stark surface of his desk, other than his nameplate and his computer monitor. So very different from the scruffy clothes and longish hair she remembered from their school days. And she'd bet those motorcycle boots were long gone, probably replaced by some kind of shiny dress shoes.

Maybe that had all been an act. Because the man she saw in front of her was every bit as disciplined as her father had been.

She shook herself, needing to gather her wits.

The only thing she should be thinking about was the here and now…and how the Clint of today could or couldn't help her daughter.

What had happened between them was in the past. It was over. And, as Clint had said, what they should be concentrating on was Chelsea.

So that's what Jessi was going to do.

If, for some reason, she judged that he couldn't help in her daughter's recovery, then she would call, write letters, parade in front of the hospital with picket signs, if necessary. And she would keep on doing it, until someone found her a doctor who could.

CHAPTER TWO

CLINT FORCED HIMSELF to stare over her shoulder rather than at the mouthwatering jiggle of her ass. The woman was no longer the stick-thin figure he'd known once upon a time. Instead, she boasted soft curves that flowed down her body like gentle ocean swells and made his hands itch to mold and explore.

Forget it, jerk. You're here for one thing only. To help Jessi's daughter and others like her.

No one had been more shocked than he'd been to realize the beautiful woman sitting across from him, worry misting her deep green eyes, was none other than the girl he'd lusted after in school.

The one he'd kissed in a rare moment of weakness, her tears triggering every protective instinct in his body.

The woman he'd handed off to the boy she'd really wanted—the one she'd married.

Unfortunately for Clint, he still didn't seem to be immune to her even after all these years.

He'd wanted to protect her.

Only he hadn't been able to back then. He couldn't now.

The only thing he could do was his job.

They reached Chelsea's room, and he shoved aside a new ache in his gut. The one that had struck when he'd realized the young woman's age was close enough to a certain deadly encounter to make him wonder whose she was.

Three months earlier and this story could have had a different ending.

No. It couldn't.

He'd done what he'd had to do back then—left—and he had no regrets.

Jessi glanced back and caught his look, her brows arching in question.

Okay, maybe he had one regret.

But it was too late to do anything about that now.

His fingers tightened on Chelsea's chart, and he started to push through the door, but Jessi stopped him. "I've been hearing things about the VA hospitals, Clint. You need to know up front that if I feel like she's not getting the treatment she needs here, I'll put her somewhere else."

His insides turned into a hard ball. He cared about his patients. All of them. No matter what the bean counters in Washington recommended or the hospital administration at whatever unit he was currently assigned to said or did, he treated his patients as if they were his comrades in arms...which they were. "It doesn't matter what you've heard. As long as I'm here, she'll get the best I have."

"But what if the hospital rules tell you to—?"

One side of his mouth went up. "Jessi May, always worried about something. Since when have you known me to play by anyone's rules?" A question they both knew the answer to, since he'd challenged almost every regulation their high school had been able to come up with.

"Would you please stop calling me that?"

His smile widened. "Is it a rule?"

"No." Her whole demeanor softened, and she actually laughed. "Because it'll just make you worse."

"I rest my case."

A nurse walked down the hallway, throwing them a curious look and reminding him of the serious issues Jessi was facing.

He took a step back. "Are you ready?"

"I think so."

Clint entered the room first, holding the door open for her.

Sitting in a chair by the window, his patient stared out across the lawn, not even acknowledging their presence. Hell, how could he not have seen the resemblance between the two women?

Chelsea had the same blond hair, the same pale, haunted features that her mother had once had. Only there was no way the young woman before him today could have survived basic training while maintaining that raw edge of vulnerability, so it was new. A result of her PTSD.

It affected people differently. Some became wounded and tortured, lashing out at themselves.

And some became impulsive and angry. Hitting out at others.

Clint wasn't sure which was worse, although as a teenager with a newly broken pinkie finger, he could have told you right off which he preferred.

Only he'd never told anyone about his finger. Or about his father.

And when he'd found Jessi crying outside the school building because of something her own father had done… he'd thought the worst. Only to have relief sweep through his system when it had been something completely different.

He drew a careful breath. "Hi, Chelsea. Do you remember me from earlier today?"

No reaction. The waif by the window continued to stare. He glanced at her chart again to remind himself of the medications Dr. Cordoba had prescribed.

He made a note to lower the dosage to see if it had any effect. He wanted to help Chelsea cope, not turn her into a zombie.

Jessi went over to her daughter and dropped to her knees, taking the young woman's hands in hers and looking up at her. "Hi, sweetheart. How are you?"

"I want to go home." The words were soft. So soft, Clint almost missed them.

Jessi hadn't, though. Her chin wobbled for a second, before she drew her spine up. "I want that, too, baby. More than anything. But you're not ready. You know you're not."

"I know." The response was just as soft. She turned to look back out the window, as if tuning out anything that didn't get her what she wanted.

Clint knew Chelsea's reaction was a defense mechanism, but having her own daughter shut her out had to shred Jessi's insides even though she was absolutely doing what was right for Chelsea.

He pulled up a chair and sat in front of the pair, forcing himself to keep his attention focused on his patient and not her mother. "I'm going to adjust some of your medications, Chelsea. Would that be okay?"

The girl sighed, but she did turn her head slightly to acknowledge she'd heard him. "Whatever you think is best."

He spent fifteen minutes watching the pair interact, making notes and comparing his observations with what he'd read of her past behavior.

She'd slashed her wrists. Jessi had found her bleeding in the bathtub and had fashioned tourniquets out of two scarves—quick thinking that had saved her daughter's life.

A couple of pints of blood later, they'd avoided permanent brain and organ damage.

Unfortunately, the infusion hadn't erased the emotional damage that had come about as a result of what her chart said was months spent in captivity.

Trauma—any trauma—had to be processed mentally and emotionally. Some people seemed to escape unscathed, letting the memory of the event roll off their backs. Others were crushed beneath it.

And others pretended they didn't give a damn.

Even when they did.

Like him?

Jessi had coaxed Chelsea over to the bed and sat next to her, arm draped around her shoulders, still talking to her softly. He got up and laid a hand on her shoulder.

"I'll give you a few minutes. Stop in and talk to me before you leave the hospital." He didn't add the word *okay* or allow his voice to change tone at the end of the phrase, because he didn't want to make it seem like a request. Not because he wasn't sure she'd honor it, but part of him wondered if she'd head back to the front desk and demand to have another doctor assigned to the case.

Clint had to somehow break the tough news to Jessi that she was stuck with him for the next couple of months or for however long Chelsea was here. There just wasn't anyone else.

So it was up to him to convince her that he could help her daughter, if she gave him a chance. Not hard, since he believed it himself. Clint had dealt with all types of soldiers in crisis, both male and female, something Dr. Cordoba had not. It was part of the reason Clint had agreed to this assignment. His rotations didn't keep him anywhere for more than six months at a time. Surely that would be long enough to treat Chelsea or at least come up with a plan for how to proceed.

If he'd known one of Dr. Cordoba's toughest cases was Jessi Spencer's daughter, though, he wouldn't have been quite so quick to agree to return to his hometown.

Being here was dangerous on a number of levels.

Jessi's not the girl you once knew.

He sensed it. She was stronger than she'd been in school. She'd had to be after being widowed at a young age and

raising a daughter on her own. And according to the list-
ing on Chelsea's chart, Jessi was now an ER physician.
You didn't deal with trauma cases all day long without
having a cast-iron stomach and a tough emotional outlook.

He'd seen a touch of that toughness in his office. Her
eyes had studied him, but had given nothing away, unlike
the Jessi of his past, who'd worn her heart on her sleeve.

Just as well. He was here to treat the daughter, not take
up where he'd left off with the mother. Not that he'd "left
off" with her. He'd had a one-night stand and had then
made sure her beau had known that to win her heart he
had to be willing to give up his dreams for her.

Evidently he had.

That was one thing Clint wouldn't do. For anyone.

If he could just keep that in mind for the next couple
of months, he'd be home free. And if he was able to help
Chelsea get the help she needed while he was at it, that
was icing on the cake.

He corrected himself. No, not just the icing. It was the
whole damn cake. And that was what he needed to focus
on.

Anything else would be a big mistake.

"And how long will that be?" Jessi's mouth opened, then
snapped back shut, before trying again. "I don't want Chelsea's next doctor to give up on her like..."

Her voice faded away as the reality of what she'd been
about to say swept through her: *Like Dr. Cordoba did.
Like Chelsea's father did when he took off into the night.*

"Are you talking about Dr. Cordoba?"

She blinked. Had he read her mind? "Yes."

"He didn't give up on her." His voice softened. "His
wife is very ill. He had to take a job that allows him to be
home with her as much as possible. He couldn't do that

and continue working long hours here. He knew his patients deserved more than that."

Oh, God. Her ire at the other doctor dissolved in a heartbeat. She'd been so caught up in her own problems that she hadn't even stopped to think that maybe he had been dealing with things that were every bit as bad as hers were. Maybe even worse. "I..." She swallowed. "I don't know what to say. I'm so sorry."

The events of the past months were suddenly too much for her, and her heart pounded, her stomach churned.

Please, no. Not now.

She'd had two panic attacks since Chelsea's hospitalization, so she recognized the signs.

Pressing a hand to her middle, she tried to force back the nausea and took a few careful breaths.

"I thought you should know." Clint leaned forward. "If you're worried about me suddenly taking off, don't be. I'll give you plenty of notice."

This time.

The words hung in the air between them, and for a horrible, soul-stealing second she thought he was hinting for her not to get her hopes up.

"I'm not expecting you to stay forever." The sensation in her chest and stomach grew, heat crawling up her neck and making her ears ring. Her vision narrowed to a pinpoint. And then it was too late to stop it. "I think I'm going..."

She lurched to her feet and somehow made it through the door and to the first stall in the restroom before her gut revolted in a violent spasm, and she threw up. She'd been running on coffee and pure adrenaline for the past several weeks, and she hadn't eaten breakfast that morning. The perfect set-up for an attack.

That had to be the reason. Not finding Clint sitting behind that desk.

Again and again, her stomach heaved, mingling with tears of frustration.

When she finally regained control over herself, she flushed the toilet with shaking hands before going to the sink, bending down to rinse her mouth and splash water over her face. She blindly reached for the paper-towel dispenser, only to have some kind of cloth pressed into her hand.

Holding the fabric tightly to her face and wishing she could blot away the past two months as easily as the moisture, she sucked down a couple more slow breaths, her heart rate finally slowing to some semblance of normality.

"Thank you." She lifted her head, already knowing who she'd find when she opened her eyes. "You shouldn't be in here."

"Why? Because it's against the rules? I thought we'd already sorted all that out." He added a smile. "Besides, I wanted to make sure you were okay."

The words swirled with bitter familiarity through her head. They were the same ones he'd said the night of their high-school graduation ceremony when she'd suddenly veered away from the rows of chairs and rushed out into the parking lot and then down to a nearby creek. Thankfully neither her dad nor mom had seen her. And an hour and a half later, when the ceremony had been over and the reception had been in full swing, she'd returned. With the lie that Clint had told her to use trembling on her tongue… that she'd been sick with nerves.

Her dad had bought it, just like Clint had said he would.

Only when she'd said it, it had no longer been a lie, because she had felt sick. Not because of nerves, but because the boy she'd always wanted—the boy she'd lost her virginity to—would soon be on his way to the airport, headed for boot camp. Leaving her behind forever.

"It's just the shock of everything."

"I know."

She shivered and wrapped her arms around herself. Clint made no effort to take off his jacket and drape it around her. It was a good thing, because she'd probably dissolve into a puddle all over again if he did.

"Have you eaten recently?"

"What?"

"I get the feeling you're running on fumes along with a heaped dose of stress. Which is probably why—" he nodded at the closed stall "—that just happened."

Leave it to him to point out the obvious. "I can eat later."

He nodded. "Yes. Or you could eat while we go over some treatment options. I skipped breakfast this morning and could use something, as well. Besides, some carbs will help settle your stomach."

Before she knew it, she found herself in the hospital cafeteria with a toasted bagel and a cup of juice sitting in front of her.

A hint of compassion in his voice as he detailed the treatments he'd like to try told her this wasn't going to be an easy fix. It was something Chelsea would be dealing with for the rest of her life. He just wanted to give her the tools she needed to do that successfully.

It was what Jessie wanted, as well. More than anything. As a mom, she wanted to be able to make things better, to take away her daughter's pain. But she couldn't. She had to trust that Clint knew what he was doing.

He certainly sounded capable.

"And what if she tries to do something to herself?" She set the bagel back down on the plate, unable to leave the subject alone.

"I'll take steps to avoid the possibility." He steepled his fingers and met her gaze with a steadiness that unnerved her. The man was intimidating, even though she knew he wasn't trying to be. Despite his reassurances, she still wasn't convinced Clint was the man for the job. Especially considering their history—which, granted, wasn't much of one. On his side, anyway.

What other option did she have, though? An institution? Bring her home and hope Chelsea didn't try to take her life again?

No. She couldn't risk there being a next time.

She'd do anything it took to help bring her daughter back from wherever she was. That included seeing Clint every day for the rest of her life and reliving what they'd done by the bank of that creek.

Decision made.

"I want you to keep me informed of every move you make."

One brow quirked. Too late she realized he could have taken her words the wrong way. But he didn't throw a quick comeback, like he might have done in days gone by. Instead, he simply said the words she needed to hear most: "Don't worry, Jessi. Even if we have to break every rule in the book, we're going to pull her through this."

And as much as the word *we* made something inside her tingle to life, it was that other statement that reached out and grabbed her. The one that said the old Clint was still crouched inside that standard issue haircut and neat-as-a-pin desk. It was there in his eyes. The glowing intensity that said, despite outward appearances, he hadn't turned into a heartless bureaucrat after years of going through proper channels.

He was a rule-breaker. He always had been. And just like his bursting into the ladies' restroom unannounced, it gave her hope, along with a sliver of fear.

She knew from experience he wasn't afraid to break anything that got in the way of what he wanted. She just had to make sure one of those "things" wasn't her heart.

CHAPTER THREE

JESSI HAD JUST finished suturing an elbow laceration and was headed in to pick up her next chart when a cry of pain came from the double bay doors of the emergency entrance.

"Ow! It hurts!"

A man holding a little girl in his arms lurched into the waiting area, his face as white as the linoleum flooring beneath his feet. The child's frilly pink party dress had a smear of dirt along one side of it, as did her arm and one side of her face. That had Jessi moving toward the pair. The other cases in the waiting room at the moment were minor illnesses and injuries.

The man's wild eyes latched on to her, taking in the stethoscope around her neck. "Are you a doctor?"

"Yes. How can I help?"

"We were at a… She fell…" The words tumbled out of his mouth, nothing making sense. Especially since the girl's pained cries were making the already stricken expression on his face even worse.

She tried to steer him in the right direction. "She fell. Is this your daughter?"

"Yes. She fell off a trampoline at a friend's house. It's her leg."

Like with many fun things about childhood—climbing trees, swimming in the lake, riding a bike—danger lurked around every corner, ready to strike.

Jessi brushed a mass of blond curls off the girl's damp face and spoke to her. "What's your name?"

"Tammy," she said between sobs.

She maintained eye contact with her little charge. "Tammy, I know your leg must hurt terribly. We're going to take you back and help fix it." She motioned to one of the nurses behind the admission's desk. Gina immediately came toward them with a clipboard.

The girl nodded, the volume of her cries going down a notch.

"Let's take her into one of the exam rooms, while Nurse Stanley gets some information."

It wasn't standard protocol—they were supposed to register all admissions unless there was a life-threatening injury—but right now Jessi wanted to take away not only the child's pain but the father's, as well.

Maybe Clint wasn't the only one who knew how to break a few rules.

But she had to. She recognized that look of utter terror and helplessness on the dad's face. She'd felt the same paralyzing fear as she'd crouched in the bathtub with her daughter, blood pouring out of Chelsea's veins. She'd sent out that same cry for help. To God. To the universe. To anyone who would listen.

And like the distraught father following her to a treatment room, she'd been forced to place her child in the hands of a trained professional and pray they could fix whatever was wrong. Because it was something beyond her own capabilities.

But what if it was also beyond the abilities of the people you entrusted them to?

Raw fear pumped back into her chest, making her lungs ache.

Stop it.

She banished Clint and Chelsea from her thoughts and

concentrated on her job. This little girl needed her, and she had to have her head in the game if she wanted to help her.

"Which leg is it?" she asked the father.

"Her right. It's her shin."

"Did she fall on the ground? Or which part of the trampoline?"

She asked question after question, gathering as much information as she could in order to narrow the steps she'd need to take to determine the exact nature of the injury.

Gina followed them into the room and was already writing furiously, even though the nurse hadn't voiced a single question. That could come later.

"Set her on the table."

As soon as cold metal touched the girl's leg, she let out an ear-piercing shriek that quickly melted back into sobs.

As a mother, it wrenched at her heart, but Jessi couldn't let any of that affect what she did next. Things would get worse for Tammy before they got better, because Jessi had to make sure she knew what she was dealing with.

"Gina, can you stay and get the rest of the information from Mr...?" She paused and glanced at the girl's father.

"Lawrence. Jack Lawrence."

"Thank you." She turned back to her nurse. "Can you do that while I call Radiology?"

Once she'd made the call, she made short work of getting the girl's vitals, talking softly to her as she went about her job. When she slid the girl's dress up a little way, she spied a dark blue contusion forming along her shin and saw a definite deformation of the tibia. The bone had separated. Whether they could maneuver the ends back in place without surgery would depend on what the X-rays showed.

Within fifteen minutes, one of the radiology techs had whisked the five-year-old down the hall on a stretcher, her father following close behind. His expression had gone from one of fear to hope. Sometimes just knowing it wasn't all up to you as a parent, that there were others willing to pitch in, made a little of the weight roll off your shoulders.

So why did she still feel buried beneath tons of rubble?

Because Chelsea's injury went beyond the physical to the very heart of who she was. And Jessi wasn't sure Clint—or anyone else—could repair it. There was no splint or cast known to man that could heal a broken spirit.

A half hour later Tammy and her father were back in the exam room, and an orthopedist had arrived to take over the case. The urge to bend down and kiss the little girl's cheek came and went. She held back a little smile. She didn't need to break *all* the rules. Some of them were there for a reason.

Hopefully, Clint knew which ones to follow and which ones to break.

He did. She sensed it.

He wouldn't go beyond certain professional boundaries. Which meant he would try to keep their past in the past. If one of them stepped over the line, he'd remove himself from Chelsea's case.

Should she talk to Chelsea about what had happened down at the creek—tell her she'd gone to school with Clint? Not necessary. He appeared to have a plan. Besides, if she heaped anything else on her daughter, she might hunker further down into whatever foxhole she'd dug for herself. She needed to give Clint enough time to do his job.

"Jessi?" Gina, the nurse from the earlier, caught her just as she was leaving her patient's room. "You have a phone call on line two."

"Okay, thanks." It must be her mom, confirming their dinner date for tonight. She'd promised to update her on Chelsea's condition, something that made her feel ill. With her father gone, Jessi and Chelsea were all her mother had left. And though her mother was no longer taking antidepressants, she'd been forgetful lately, which Jessi hoped was just from the stress of her only granddaughter's illness.

Going to the reception desk, she picked up the phone and punched the lit button. "Hello?"

Instead of the bright, happy tones of her mother, she encountered something a couple of octaves lower. "Jess?"

She gulped. "Yes?"

"Clint here."

As if she hadn't already recognized the sound of his voice. Still, her heart leaped with fear. "Is something wrong with Chelsea?"

"No. Do you have a minute? I'd like to take care of some scheduling."

"Scheduling?"

A low, incredibly sexy-sounding hum came through the phone that made something curl in her belly.

"I want us to talk every day."

"Every day?"

About Chelsea, you idiot! And what was with repeating everything he said?

"Yes. Our schedules are probably both hectic, but we can do it by phone, if necessary."

"Oh. Okay." Was he saying he didn't want to meet with her in person? That he'd rather do all of this by phone? She had no idea, but she read off her schedule for the next five days.

A grunt of affirmation came back, along with, "I'll also want to meet with you and Chelsea together."

"Why?"

"Didn't Dr. Cordoba have family sessions with you?"

She shook her head, only realizing afterwards that he couldn't see it. "No, although he mentioned wanting to try that further down the road."

"I believe in getting the family involved as soon as possible, since you'll be the one working with her once she's discharged."

Discharged. The most beautiful word Chelsea had heard in weeks. And Clint made it sound like a reality, rather than just a vague possibility. So he really was serious about doing everything he could to make sure treatment was successful.

A wave of gratitude came over her and a knot formed in her throat. "Thank you, Clint. For being willing to break the rules."

Was she talking about with Chelsea? Or about their time together all those years ago.

"You're welcome, Jess. For what it's worth, I think Chelsea is very lucky to have you."

Her next words came out before she was aware of them forming in her head. But she meant them with all her heart. "Ditto, Clint. I think Chelsea and I are the lucky ones."

"I'll call you."

With that intimate-sounding promise, he said goodbye, and the phone clicked in her ear, telling her he'd hung up. She gripped the receiver as tightly as she could, all the while praying she was doing the right thing. She was about to allow Clint back into her orbit—someone who'd once carried her to the peak of ecstasy and then tossed her into the pit of despair without a second glance. But what choice did she have, really?

She firmed her shoulders. No, there was always a choice. She may have made the wrong one when she'd been on the cusp of womanhood, but she was smarter now. Stronger. She could—and would—keep her emotions in check. If not for her own sake, then for her daughter's.

CHAPTER FOUR

THE FIRST FAMILY counseling session was gearing up to be a royal disaster.

Jessi came sliding into Clint's office thirty minutes late, out of breath, face flushed, wispy strands of hair escaping from her clip.

He swallowed back a rush of emotion. She'd looked just like this as she'd stood to her feet after they'd made love. He'd helped her brush her hair back into place, combing his fingers through the strands and wishing life could be different for him.

But it couldn't. Not then. And not now.

"Sorry. We had an emergency at the hospital, and I had to stay and help."

"No problem." He stood. "I have another patient in a half hour, so we'll need to make this a quick session."

"Poor Chelsea. I feel awful. I'm off tomorrow, though, so I'll come and spend the day with her."

When they walked into Chelsea's room, the first thing he noticed was that the lunch she'd been served an hour ago was still on a tray in front of her, untouched. At the sight of them, though, she seemed to perk up in her seat, shoveling a bite of mashed potatoes into her mouth and making a great show of chewing.

Manipulating. He'd seen signs of it earlier when he'd

tried to coax her to talk about things that didn't involve the weather.

Her throat worked for a second with the food still pouched inside one cheek. She ended up having to wash the potatoes down with several gulps of water. She sat there, breathing as hard as her mother had been when she'd arrived a few moments ago.

"Enjoying your meal?" he asked, forcing his voice to remain blasé. So much for showing Jessi how good he was at his job.

As if this was even about him.

He ground his teeth as his frustration shifted to himself.

Chelsea shrugged. Another bite went in—albeit a much smaller one this time.

Not polite to talk with my mouth full, was the inference.

Well, she'd run out of the stuff eventually. And since she was pretty thin already, he was all for anything that would get food into her system. That was one of the comments on the sheet in her file. She didn't eat much, unless someone wanted to interact with her in some way. The staff had taken to coming to her room and loitering around, straightening things and making small talk. It was a surefire way to get that fork moving from plate to mouth.

He decided to give her a little more time.

Jessi stood there, looking a little lost by her daughter's lack of greeting. He sent her a nod of reassurance and motioned her to sit in one of the two nearby chairs and joined her.

"Let's go ahead and get started, if that's okay with you, Chelsea."

Chew, chew, chew.

She moved on to her green beans without a word. Okay, if that's the way she wanted to play it, he'd go right along with it.

He turned to Jessi, sorry for what he was about to do,

but if anything could break through her daughter's wall it might be having to face some hard, unpleasant subjects. "Since Chelsea's busy, why don't you tell me what led her to being here."

Right on cue, Jessi's eyes widened. "You mean about the day I called…"

"Yes."

Her throat moved a couple of times, swallowing, probably her way of either building up the courage to talk about the suicide attempt or to refuse.

"Well, I—I called Chelsea's cell phone to let her know I was coming home early. It rang and rang before finally going over to voice mail. I was going to stop and pick up some Thai food—her favorite…" Jessi's eyes filled with tears. "I decided to go straight home instead, so we could go out to eat together. When I got there… Wh-when I got to the house, I—"

"Stop." Chelsea's voice broke through, though she was still staring down, a green bean halfway to her mouth. "Don't make her talk about it."

Whether the young woman wanted to spare her mother's feelings or her own, Clint wasn't sure. "What would you like to discuss instead, then?"

There was a long pause. Then she said, "What you hope to accomplish by keeping me here."

"It's not about us, Chelsea. It's about you."

"Where's Dr. Cordoba?" Her head finally came up, and her gaze settled on him.

"He went to work somewhere else."

"Because of me." The words came out as a whisper.

Clint shook his head. "No, of course not. He made the decision for personal reasons. It had nothing to do with you."

Jessi's chest rose and fell as she took a quick breath. "We all just want to help, honey."

"Everything I touch turns to ashes."

"No." Jessi glanced at him, then scooted closer to her daughter, reaching out to stroke her hair. "You've been through a lot in the past several months, but you're not alone."

"I am, Mom. You have no idea. You all think I'm suffering from PTSD, because of my time in that camp, don't you? Dr. Cordoba did. But I'm not."

Clint glanced at Jessi, a frown on his face. "You tried to take your life, Chelsea. Something made you think life wasn't worth living."

The girl's shoulders slumped.

"Does this have to do with your pregnancy?"

Two sets of female eyes settled on him in shock.

Hell. Jessi hadn't known?

It was right there in Chelsea's medical chart that her physical exam had revealed she'd given birth or had had a miscarriage at some point. He'd just assumed...

His patient went absolutely rigid. "I want her to leave. Now."

"But, Chelsea..." Jessi's voice contained a note of pleading.

"Now." The girl's voice rose in volume. "Now, now. *Now!*"

Jessi careened back off her chair and stumbled from the room as her daughter's wails turned to full-fledged screams of pain. She was tearing at her hair, her food flung across the room. Clint pressed the call button for the nurse and between the two of them they were able to administer a sedative, putting an end to Chelsea's hysterical shrieks. Her muscles finally went limp and her eyes closed. He stood staring down at her bed for a few moments, a feeling of unease settling over him as it had each time he'd met with Chelsea. There was something here. Something more than what was revealed in her records.

And it involved that pregnancy. She'd been calm until the moment the subject had come up.

It was time to do a little more digging. But for now he had to go out there and face Jessi. And somehow come up with something to say that wouldn't make things worse than they already were.

"I didn't know."

Clint came toward her as she leaned against the wall twenty feet away from Chelsea's door. Her stomach had roiled within her as the nurse had rushed into the room and the screams had died down to moans, before finally fading away to nothing. All she wanted to do was throw up, just like she had during a previous visit, but she somehow held it together this time.

"I'm sorry, Jess." Clint scrubbed a hand through his hair, not touching her. "I'd assumed she told you."

"She hasn't told me anything. Could it have been while she was a prisoner?"

"I'm not sure. This is the most emotion I've seen from her in the past week. We hit a nerve, though. So that's a good thing."

"I can't imagine what she went through." She leaned her head against the wall and stared at the ceiling.

Chelsea's convoy had been ambushed during a night patrol by enemy forces disguised as police officers. The group had been held for four months. Chelsea had said they'd all been separated and interrogated, but she'd had no idea one of the prisoners had died until she and the rest of those rescued had been flown home.

Jessi sighed and turned back to look at him. "The army debriefed her, but I was never told what she said, and I—I was afraid to press her too much. She seemed to be doing fine. Maybe that in itself was a warning sign."

"There was no way you could have known what she was going to do." Clint pushed a strand of hair off her cheek.

She wasn't sure she could stand seeing her daughter in this much pain week after week. And a pregnancy...

Had her daughter been raped during her captivity? The army had said there was no evidence of that, but then again Chelsea wasn't exactly a fount of information. "I think I'm doing more harm than good by going in there with you."

"Let's see how it goes for the next week, okay? Chelsea was admitted under a suicide watch. That gives you permission to make decisions regarding her health care. She could still open up."

"She doesn't even want me here, Clint. You heard her." Jessi's head still reverberated with her daughter's cries for her to get out.

"That was the shock talking. She didn't expect me to ask that particular question. At least she's getting it out, rather than bottling it all up inside."

His eyes narrowed as he looked at her face. "How long's it been since you've done something that hasn't revolved around your job or Chelsea?"

She thought for a second. "I can't remember."

"The last thing she needs is for you to break down as well, which is where you're headed if you don't take some down time."

She knew he was right. She'd felt like she'd been standing on the edge of a precipice for weeks now, with no way to back away from it.

Before she could say anything, he went on. "You said you're off tomorrow. Why don't you go out and do something fun? Something you enjoy?"

"I need to spend the day here with Chelsea."

"No. You don't. She'll understand. It might not be a bad idea to give her a day to think through what just happened."

She hesitated. "I don't even know what I'd do." Chelsea might need a day to think, but the last thing Jessi wanted to do was sit at home and let her brain wander down dark paths.

"Tell you what. I don't have anything pressing tomorrow. Why don't we do something together? It's fair season. There's probably something going on in one of the nearby counties."

"Oh, but I couldn't. Chelsea—"

"Will be fine."

Conflicting emotions swept through her. The possibility of spending the day with Clint dangled before her in a way that was far too attractive. "I'm not sure..."

"Is it because I'm her doctor?"

"Yes." He'd given her the perfect excuse, and she grabbed at it with both hands.

"That can be remedied."

Panic sizzled through her. He'd hinted once before that he might drop her daughter's case.

"No. I want you."

He paused, then shook his head and dragged his fingertips across her cheek. "Then you have to take care of yourself."

She nodded, unable to look away from his eyes as they locked on her face. Several emotions flicked through them, none of them decipherable.

"I'll try."

"How about I check the local schedules and see if I can find something for us to do? Something that doesn't involve a hospital."

Guilt rose in her throat, but at a warning glance from him she forced it back down. "Okay."

He nodded and let his hand fall back to his side. "Are you going to be okay tonight?"

Was he asking her that as a psychiatrist or as a man?

It didn't matter. The last thing she wanted was to jeopardize her working relationship with the one man who might be able to get through to her daughter. She needed to keep this impersonal. Professional. Even though his touch brought back a whole lot of emotions she hadn't felt in twenty-two years.

But she had to keep them firmly locked away. Somehow.

"I'll be fine. Just call if there's any change, okay?" She was proud of the amount of conviction she'd inserted into her voice.

"I will. I'm off at ten, but the hospital knows how to reach me if there's a problem." He took a card from his desk and wrote something on the back of it, then handed it to her. "I'll give you a yell in the morning, but until then, here's my cell phone number. Call me if you need me."

If you need me.

Terrifying words, because she already did. More than she should. But she wouldn't call. No matter how much that little voice inside her said to do just that.

CHAPTER FIVE

CLINT STEPPED ONTO the first row of metal bleachers and held his hand out for her. Grasping his fingers, and letting him maneuver through the crowd of seated spectators, they went to the very top, where a metal brace across the end provided a place for their backs to rest.

She watched the next horse in line prance into the arena, ears pricked forward in anticipation. Three fifty-five-gallon drums had been laid out to form a familiar triangle.

Barrel racing.

The speed event looked deceptively easy, but if a horse knocked over a barrel as it went around it, the rider received a five-second penalty, enough to cost a winning ribbon.

"I used to do this, you know. Run barrels."

"I know you did."

Her head swiveled to look at the man sitting next to her, completely missing the horse's take-off.

"You did?"

He smiled. "I came to the fair on occasion. Watched a few of the 4-H events."

The thought of Clint sitting on one of these very bleachers, watching her compete, was unnerving. How would she have missed him with the way he'd dressed back then? He hadn't exactly looked the part of an emerging cowboy.

Exactly. She would have noticed him.

Which meant he'd never actually seen her race. She settled back into place.

"I didn't realize you were interested in 4-H."

His gaze went back to the arena. "I wasn't."

Something about the way he'd said that...

"Do you still have your trophy?" He was still looking straight ahead, thankfully, but her gasp sounded like a gunshot to her ears, despite the noise going on around her.

The metal brace behind her groaned as more people leaned against it. Jessi eased some of her weight off it.

"How did you know I...?" She'd only won one trophy in all her years of entering the event.

"I happened to be in the vicinity that day."

How did one *happen* to be in the vicinity of the fair? It spanned a large area. And the horse arena wasn't exactly next to the carnival rides or food.

"You saw me run?"

"I saw a lot of people compete."

Okay, that explained it. "So you came out to all the horse events?"

"Not all of them. I had a few friends who did different things."

Like run barrels? She didn't think so. Neither did she remember him hanging out with any of her 4-H friends. And the only year she'd won the event had been as a high school senior.

The next horse—a splashy brown and white paint—came in, and she fixed her attention on it, although her mind was going at a million miles an hour. The rider directed the horse in a tight circle near the starting area and then let him go. The animal's neck stretched forward as he raced toward the first barrel, tail streaming out behind him.

"Here!" the rider called as they reached the drum, using her voice along with her hands and legs to guide the horse around the turn. She did the same for the second and third barrels and then the pair raced back in a straight line until they crossed where the automatic timer was set up. Nineteen point two three seconds.

The announcer repeated the time, adding that it put the horse and rider into second place.

Clint leaned closer, his scent washing over her at almost exactly the same time as his arm brushed hers. The dual assault made her mind blank out for a second. So much so that she almost missed his question. "I always wondered. Why do some of them start with the left barrel rather than the one on the right?"

Play it cool, Jessi.

"B-because horses have a dominant side, kind of like being right- or left-handed."

"Interesting. So your horse was right-handed?"

She swallowed. So he *had* seen her. She'd hoped maybe he'd heard that she'd won from a friend, rather than having been there in the flesh. What did it matter? So he'd seen her race. No big deal.

But it was. And she had no idea why.

"Yes, she was."

Neither of the next two horses beat the time of the leader. Despite her wariness at coming out today, and her horror at realizing he'd watched her the day of her win, she could feel the muscles in her body relaxing. He'd been right to suggest she take a day off.

A *real* day off.

"Do you think Chelsea—?"

"The hospital will call me if they need me. We're both off duty today."

She frowned. "She's my daughter, Clint. I can't help but worry about her."

"I'm not asking you to put her from your mind. I'm asking you to enjoy your day. It's what she would want."

She sighed. "She did seem happy when I told her where I was going." Jessi had insisted on stopping to see Chelsea before they'd left, although she hadn't told her that she and Clint were going together.

"Exactly." He bumped her with his shoulder again. "And she's probably going to ask what you did. So let's make it good."

Jessi's eyes widened. How was she supposed to respond to that?

She was still trying to figure it out when she heard a weird screech of metal, then Clint's arm was suddenly behind her, crushing her tightly against him.

"Hold on!"

She thought at first it was because a new horse had started the course, but then she sensed something falling, followed by screams.

When she glanced back, she saw that the metal support had broken free—probably from the weight of everyone leaning against it—and was dangling from the far side of the bleachers. And on the ground...

Oh, Lord. Fifteen feet below them were five people who'd evidently tumbled backward off the top seat when the structure had given way. Others were now on their feet in a panic, trying to rush down the stands to get to the ground. One person tripped and landed on another spectator a few rows down.

"Stay here," Clint muttered.

Like hell. "I'm coming with you. I'm a doctor, too, remember?"

Someone in the judges' booth called over the loudspeakers, asking for everyone to remain calm. And also asking for medical assistance.

Clint cautiously made his way down, trying to make sure he didn't trample on anyone, and again holding her hand as he took one step at a time.

By the time they reached the bottom they could hear a siren that cut off just as it reached the wide dirt aisle that separated the main arena from campers and horse trailers. The crowd opened a path to let it through.

One of the victims was now on her feet and waving away offers for help. Another person had disappeared, evidently also unhurt. But the remaining three were still on the ground, although one was sitting up, holding his leg.

"I'm a doctor," Clint said to him. "Can you hold on for a minute while we check the others?"

"Go," the man said, his thin, wiry frame and rugged clothing suggesting he was a farmer or someone who worked with livestock.

Jessi motioned that she'd take the far patient, a woman who was on her side, moaning, while Clint took the last remaining patient, a child, who was writhing on the ground and crying. They pushed through layers of people who wanted to help.

"I'm a doctor, let me through," she said to a man who was kneeling next to the woman. The man backed up to make room in the tight circle.

The EMT vehicle stopped and two medical workers jumped from the back just as Jessi crouched near her patient. The woman was conscious but obviously in a lot of pain.

"Where does it hurt?"

"Brandi," she gasped, ignoring the question and trying to roll onto her back, only to stop with a moan. "My daughter. Where's Brandi?"

Jessi glanced to the side, but couldn't see Clint through the bodies of onlookers, but his patient had looked to be a little girl.

"How old is your daughter?"

"She…she's five. Pink shorts." Talking was an obvious struggle for her.

That had to be Clint's patient.

"Someone's helping her right now. Where does it hurt?"

"M-My ribs. It hurts to breathe."

Jessi did a quick rundown of the woman's vitals. Everything seemed good, except for a marked tenderness on her right side. "Did you hit your head at all?"

"No. Just landed flat on my side. I couldn't get up."

One of the emergency services workers knelt beside her. "What have you got?"

Jessi glanced at the man, who looked to be almost as young as Chelsea. "Possible rib fractures." She read off the woman's vitals. "How's the little girl next to us?"

"Fractured wrist, but she looks good to go."

Jessi's patient broke down in tears. "Is that her? My daughter?"

It was amazing someone hadn't been more seriously injured or even killed in that fall. But luckily the bleachers had been built on dirt rather than a harder surface like concrete or asphalt.

She turned to the EMT. "Can you ask Dr. Marks if his patient's name is Brandi? It's her daughter, if so."

"Sure. I'll be right back."

Asking everyone to move back as he did so, she finally had a clear line of sight to Clint. He gave her a reassuring wink that made her smile.

God, how familiar that was. And it still made a jolt of electricity go through her system.

The girl was indeed Brandi, and within minutes everyone had been bundled up into two ambulances, which were creeping back between the throngs of horses and people, and soon disappeared. The sirens were off this time, probably trying not to spook the horses and risk more accidents.

Clint grasped her elbow and eased her over to the side. "They're taping off the bleachers."

Her adrenaline was just beginning to dissipate from her

system. "I felt the piece of metal give a little bit earlier, but it's been here for ages. I had no idea it could come loose."

"Just an accident."

"Thank God it wasn't worse. How about the person who fell, trying to get down?"

"Evidently they were all okay, since we didn't have any other patients."

With the excitement dying down, people were moving over to the rail next to the arena as the remaining barrel racers moved back into position.

"Do you want something to eat?"

She glanced up at him. "You can eat, after all that?"

He tweaked her chin. "They're all fine, Jess. Let's enjoy the rest of the day."

Their patients may have been fine, but Jessi wasn't so sure about herself. The memory of his hand grasping hers as he'd hauled her up the steps wound around her senses. She missed his touch. Wanted to reach over and...

The cell phone on Clint's hip buzzed. The hospital? Her whole body stiffened as dread rose up to fill her being.

Clint's system went on high alert as he put the phone to his ear.

"Marks here."

"Clinton? Clinton Marks?"

Frowning, he tried to place the feminine voice on the other end of the line. While the light Southern drawl was familiar, it definitely wasn't anyone from the hospital, because they would have called him "Doctor." If this was some telemarketer, they were about to get an earful for scaring Jessi.

And she was scared. He could read it in her stiff posture and the hands clenched at her sides.

He decided to go ultra-formal. "This is Dr. Marks."

"Well, *Dr.* Marks—" there was an air of amusement

to the voice now "—this is Abigail Spencer, Jessi's mom. Chelsea's grandmother. You remember me, don't you?"

Hell. That's why she sounded familiar.

He mouthed "Your mom" to relieve Jessi's fears, wondering why she was calling him instead of Jessi.

Jessi evidently had the same idea as he did, because she frowned and checked her phone. Maybe it was dead or something.

Clint and Jessi's dads had both been stationed at the same base, so he'd seen her parents quite a bit during his school years. His memories of Mrs. Spencer were of a kind woman with blond curls very like her daughter's and a quiet smile. So very different from his own mother's tense and fearful posture that had cropped up anytime she'd heard that front door open. Or how she would place her body in front of her son's until she had gauged what mood her husband had brought home with him. He rubbed a thumb across his pinky. His mother hadn't always been able to protect him, though.

Which was why the Spencer household had seemed so strange and alien to him. He'd never been able to shake the feeling that Jessi's mom had seen right through to the hurting kid hidden beneath a rebellious leather jacket and spiked hair. He brought his attention back to Jessi's mom as the silence over the phone grew awkward. He cleared his throat. "Of course I remember you. How are you?"

"Anxious to see my granddaughter. But Jessi told me that's not a good idea right now. I want to ask why. It's been over two months."

He didn't understand what that had to do with him, unless Jessi had used him as an excuse to deflect her visits. But whatever it was, that was between the two of them as far as he was concerned.

"I'm sorry, Mrs. Spencer. I really think you should talk to your daughter about that, because I can't discuss Chelsea's treatment. Jessi would have to give written authorization to—"

A poke to his arm made him look at the woman beside him. She shook her head.

Mrs. Spencer's voice came back down the line. "I can do better than that. Why don't you come over for dinner tonight? Jessi will be here, and we can hash all this out between the three of us." There was a pause. When her voice came back it was on the shaky side. "I'm her grandmother. Don't you think I'm entitled to know what's going on?"

"Again, that's not up to me." He felt like an utter jackass for saying those words to a woman who'd been nothing but nice to him during his time in Richmond, but Jess was staring holes right through him. "Jessi has medical power of attorney at the moment."

"She's trying to protect me, but I don't need protecting." An audible breath came through the receiver. "Won't you please come to dinner?"

There was no way he was going to walk into a situation like that without Jessi being fully aware of what was coming, and he wasn't willing to admit her daughter was standing right next to him. Not without Jess's approval. "Tell you what. Call your daughter and talk to her. If she's in agreement with me coming over tonight, I'll be glad to." How was that for admitting he had no other plans for a Friday evening?

Another poke to the arm, harder this time. "What are you doing?" she whispered.

He gave her a helpless shrug.

Unlike Jessi, he'd never married, instead throwing his whole life into helping others who were dealing with traumatic events stemming from their military service. It had been the least he could do for his dad, who, like Chelsea, had felt all alone.

"Okay, I'll do that." A quick laugh made a warning

system go off in his head. "Do you still like corned-beef brisket?"

She remembered that? He'd eaten over at their house exactly once, which was when he'd discovered how over-protective her dad was—the polar opposite of his. And he hadn't liked Clint. At all. Clint had never been invited back to the house again.

"I love brisket." Not that he thought there was a snow-ball's chance in hell that Jessi would agree to him coming over and talking about Chelsea's condition. If she'd wanted her mom to know how treatment was going, surely she would have told her by now.

"See you around seven, then."

Not quite sure how to answer that, he settled for a non-committal reply. "Thank you for the invitation, Mrs. Spen-cer."

The phone clicked off.

He met Jessi's accusing eyes. "Why did you let her in-vite you to dinner?"

As if he'd had any choice in the matter. One eyebrow went up. "I think the more important question is how did she get my number and why is she calling me, instead of you?"

"I don't know what you—"

Her phone started playing some samba beat that made him smile. Jessi groaned. "Oh, Lord. How am I going to get you out of this?"

"Don't worry about trying. I can come, if it's okay with you." Why he'd said that he had no idea.

"Hi, Mom. No, I'm…out at the fair." She licked her lips, while Clint handed money to the man in the funnel cake booth. "I know, I'm sorry. It was a spur-of-the-minute thing. A friend invited me."

She listened again, her face turning pink. "No, it's not a *guy* friend."

Pretend feathers all over his body began to ruffle and quiver in outrage as he accepted two plates from the vender. Uh…he could show her he was a guy, if she needed proof. Scratch that. She'd already seen the proof.

"Don't sound so disappointed, Mother." She rolled her eyes and glanced back at him. "You did what? How did you get his number?"

Her lips tightened, and she plopped down on a nearby bench, shutting her eyes for a second. "That's right. I forgot I left his card on the refrigerator. What were you doing at my house, anyway?"

Clint shifted beside her, uneasy about listening in on the conversation.

"Mom, you are going to spoil Cooper rotten. You know he has a weigh-in coming up."

Cooper? He set one of the plates on her lap and kept the other for himself. Did Jessi have another boyfriend? Visions of some muscle-bound hunk lounging in her bed came to mind.

No, she would have said something to him.

And exactly when had he given her the chance? He'd asked about Larry, but not about any other man who might be waiting in the wings.

"What? Clint *already* agreed to come? Wow, he sounds a little desperate, doesn't he?"

She stuck her tongue out at him, just as he took a bite of his fried cake, making him relax in his seat. "Okay, I'm about done here, so I'll start heading back that way. Love you."

He hadn't exactly agreed to go, and he was glad Jessi had heard for herself his side of the conversation. His smile widened. It would seem Mrs. Spencer could play loose and easy with rules, too.

She got off the phone and picked her cake up with a napkin he held out to her.

"Desperate, am I?" He didn't try to hide the wry tone to his voice.

"What could I do? If I said you couldn't come to dinner, she'd make up her own conclusions. And I couldn't exactly admit that you were sitting right next to me, eating funnel cake, could I?"

That part was his fault. He'd been the one to pretend they weren't together.

"So who's Cooper?" He dropped the question as if it were no big deal. Which it wasn't.

"A communal beagle," she said, as she swallowed. "Mmm...that's good stuff."

Also good was the dot of powdered sugar on her lower lip. One he was just able to refrain from licking off.

"A communal...beagle?"

Her tongue sailed across her lip, whisking away the sugar. "Okay, I guess that does sound weird. He adopted me about a year ago...came waddling up to the door and scratched on it. No one ever claimed him, so Mom and I have been caring for him between the two of us. He's on a diet. Supposedly." Stretching her legs out in front of her, she went on, "When I have to work late, Mom takes him to her house. You'll probably meet him tonight. Since you're evidently coming to dinner."

She munched down on another piece of cake, moaning in enjoyment. "That is if you still have room for food after this."

"You haven't asked me if I had plans for the evening."

Her eyes widened. "Oh, God. I'm sorry. Do you?"

"No. But I don't want to make things any harder for you than they already are." The tortured look when she'd discovered her daughter's pregnancy came back to haunt him. "I know this isn't easy, Jess."

"No, it's not." She paused, setting her food back on her plate. "Can you let me set the tone of the conversation?

Mom will just worry herself sick if she knew the extent of what Chelsea is facing. And she hasn't seemed herself recently either. She was on antidepressants for several years, so it has me worried."

He frowned, surprised by the information. But people sometimes hid their problems well. "Does she know about the suicide attempt?"

"Yes. But she wasn't there when it happened. She only knew…afterwards."

He touched her hand. "You sure you want me to come?"

"I'm not sure of anything right now. But Mom is right. Chelsea is her granddaughter. One she hasn't seen in over two months. It's time to start letting her know what's going on. I—I just want to feed her the information in bits she can process. She's been through a lot in the past five years."

Since her husband's death.

"I understand." He withdrew his hand and sat up straighter. "I'll let you answer specific questions, and I can fill in any of the medical gaps. How does that sound?"

"Perfect. Thanks so much, Clint."

Well, at least she hadn't thrown his card away. Then again, she hadn't kept it in her wallet either. "If you're done, I'll take you back to the house. I'm pretty sure you don't want us arriving in the same car."

She handed him her plate and waited until he'd thrown them both in a nearby trash receptacle to answer.

"Probably not a good idea." She smiled and stood to her feet. As they made their way back to the parking area, Clint had one thought. He hoped tonight went a whole lot better than his day had.

Jessi's plans for a relaxing evening at home looked like they were shot to hell. Between helping her mom set the table and dragging her makeup bag from her purse to touch up the dark circles under her eyes, she was getting more and more antsy. It was one thing to spend a few relaxing hours at the fair. It was another thing entirely to eat a meal with him while her mother grilled them about Chelsea's condition, which of course she would.

She'd just put the last swipe of mascara on her lashes when the doorbell rang and Cooper started up with the baying his breed was famous for. She froze, the makeup wand still in her right hand. Sucking down a breath, she quickly shoved it back in the tube, blinked at herself in the bathroom mirror and headed to get the door.

By the time she got halfway down the stairs she saw her mother had beaten her to it, apron wrapped around her waist. The door opened, and Cooper bumbled forward to greet the newcomer.

As Clint bent to pet the dog, Jessi couldn't help but stare. He'd evidently showered as well, because his hair was still damp. Dressed in a red polo shirt that hugged his shoulders and snug black jeans that hugged other—more dangerous—parts, he looked better than any funnel cake she'd ever had. He straightened and went over to kiss her mother's cheek, while Cooper continued to snuffle and groan at his ankles.

His eyes came up. Met hers across the room.

A sting of awareness rippled through her as his gaze slid over her white peasant shirt and dark-wash jeans before coming back up to her face. One side of his mouth pulled up into something that might have been a smile. Then again, it could have just as easily been classified as a modified grimace. Either way, the action caused that crease in his cheek to deepen and her heart rate to shoot through the roof.

Sexy man. Sexy smile. Stupid girl.

Hurrying the rest of the way down the stairs, she grabbed Cooper's collar and tugged him back into the house, while greeting Clint with as much nonchalance as she could muster under the circumstances. "Glad you could make it."

Not that there'd been much choice on either of their parts. Her mom had made sure of that. And right now the woman was the perfect hostess, ushering Clint in and offering him a drink, which he declined. That surprised her. He'd been such a rebel in high school that everyone had assumed that he'd played it loose and easy with alcohol, although she'd never actually seen him touch the stuff.

Her mom glanced at her in question, but Jessi shook her head. She needed all her wits about her if this evening was going to go according to plan. If she could help it, they were going to avoid talking about Chelsea as much as possible, and when her mom pressed for information, she would be honest but gloss over some of the more depressing aspects of her granddaughter's present situation. Like the fact that she either didn't want to talk about what had precipitated her suicide attempt, or she had simply blocked out that portion of her life. Who knew which it was? And it wasn't like Clint had had much time to get to the bottom of things. He'd been her doctor for, what…a little under a week?

"You look lovely," Clint said to her once her mom had gone to the kitchen to put the finishing touches on their meal. Cooper, obviously hoping for a few dropped morsels, puttered along behind her.

"Thank you." She bit her lip. "I'm really, really sorry you got caught in the middle of this."

"It's fine. I haven't had a homemade meal in…" He paused. "Well, it's been a while."

A while since someone had cooked for him? Jessi found that hard to believe. A man like Clint wouldn't have any trouble finding dates. He was even better looking now than he'd been in high school, although she never would have believed that possible. Gangly and rebellious as a teenager, he had filled out, not only physically—which was impressive enough—but he now had a maturity about him that had been lacking all those years ago. Oh, he'd made all the girls, including her, nervous wrecks back then. But as a man—well, she'd be hard pressed to say he wasn't breathtaking in a totally masculine way. From the self-assured smile to the confidence he exuded, he gave her more than a glimmer of hope that this was a man who could help her daughter.

"Have a seat," she told him. "Mom will be back any minute, and I'd like to set some quick ground rules. Like I said earlier, I haven't told her much about Chelsea's behavior—she knows about the suicide attempt, but not much about her time at the hospital. I wanted to keep it simple until I felt like there was some ho—"

Her voice cracked as an unexpected wave of emotion splashed over her, blocking the one word she wanted to believe in.

"Until you felt like there was some hope?" He finished the sentence for her. "There's always hope, Jess. I think we'll start seeing a little more progress in the coming weeks."

He shifted to face her. "Exactly what do you want me to say to your mom? I'm not comfortable with lying."

And yet he'd been the one to suggest she lie to her father about what happened after she'd run out of the gym during graduation all those years ago. To protect himself from her dad's wrath? Or to protect her?

Maybe it had been a little of both.

"I don't expect you to lie. You said there's always hope. If you could just keep that as a running theme when you talk about Chelsea, it would help Mom feel better."

"She's going to ask to see her, you know. Is there a reason you don't want her to?"

"I'm worried about her, like I told you earlier. I want to...be there when she sees Chelsea."

And I want you to have time to work your magic first. She didn't say the words, but she wanted them to be true. She trusted him. Why that was she couldn't say. She hadn't seen them interact that much. But he'd said he'd do his very best for Chelsea and she believed him. She just hoped it was enough.

Five minutes later, they were called into dinner. Cooper settled under the table with his head propped on Clint's right foot, despite all her efforts to deter him.

"He's fine," Clint said. "As long as he doesn't expect me to share any of that delicious-looking brisket."

They all laughed, and Jessi gave a quick sigh of relief. She'd half expected her mom to grill Clint on Chelsea's prognosis from the moment they sat down, but it was mostly small talk as Jessi munched lettuce leaves with nerves that were as crackly as the salad. The feared topic didn't hit until they were halfway through her mom's famed brisket, which, despite being as succulent as ever, was getting tougher and tougher for her to force down.

"Jessi tells me that she thinks Chelsea is dealing with PTSD. Is that what you're seeing, as well?"

Clint dabbed his mouth with his napkin and nodded. "We see quite a number of veterans who come back with issues related to what they've seen and done."

"Does that mean you have some ideas on how to proceed?"

Jessi's eyes jerked to his and found him watching her. She put her fork on the table as she waited for him to answer.

"We're keeping our options open at the moment. I'm still working through the notes from her previous doctor."

"That's right. I forgot you'd just moved home. What

perfect timing. Or were you just so homesick that you couldn't bear to stay away any longer?"

Jessi sucked down too much of the water she'd been sipping and choked for a second, but Clint didn't miss a beat. "Doctors are transferred to other locations on a regular basis, just like any other member of the armed forces." He gave a rueful twist of the mouth. "We both know about that, don't we?"

Way to go, Clint. Find something you have in common and use it to evade the real question.

Kind of like he'd done when she'd asked him why he had to leave the day after graduation. "I've already signed the papers, and that's when they told me to show up" had been his answer. She'd bought it at the time. But now? She had a feeling he'd just wanted to avoid her making any demands on him after their shared time together.

Which stung even more now than it had when he'd said the words.

Jessi's mom smiled back. "I'm sure you've done your share of moving, just like we did when Jessi was little." She paused then said, "I'm really glad you're back, though, and that you'll be the one treating Chelsea."

Clint's face registered surprise. "Why is that?"

Cutting into another section of her meat, her mom glanced up with a hint of sadness mixed with what looked like relief. "Because you, more than anyone, know what it's like to live with the effects of PTSD."

CHAPTER SIX

THE ROOM WAS silent for five long seconds.

Clint knew, because he counted every damn tick of the clock. He hadn't told Jessi or anyone else about his dad and the problems he'd had. Could his mom have mentioned it to Abigail or someone else from their past?

Worse, did Jessi know?

Even as the questions ducked through his cerebral cortex, looking for a believable response, he thought he saw pity flit through Jessi's eyes, although right now her mouth was hanging open in shock.

But, eventually, he had to say something. The ache in his pinky finger sprang to life, reminding him of all the reasons he'd decided to join the military and leave Jessi far behind. He clenched his fist to rid himself of the sensation and made a decision.

He was going to tell the truth. Air his dirty laundry—at least about his father. After all these years.

"Yes. I do know."

Jessi's fork clattered to her plate, and her mouth snapped shut. "Mom, I don't think that's an appropriate thing to blurt out at the dinner table."

Wounded green eyes, so like her daughter's, widened. "Oh, I'm sorry. I didn't realize. I just assumed that everyone knew—"

"It's okay," Clint said, his thumb scrubbing across the crooked joint, a habit he used as a daily reminder of why his job was so crucial. Because PTSD didn't affect just the individual soldier…it affected everyone around them, as well. "I didn't talk about my problems much. And for a long time I didn't realize that something could be done."

Jessi finally spoke up. "*You* had PTSD?"

"No. My dad did. It was back when I was in high school."

Differing emotions flickered through her eyes. Sadness. Shock. Then finally the one he'd hoped never to see: guilt.

"Clint, I—" Her tongue flicked across her lips. "You never told any of us."

"Would *you* have?"

He knew she'd catch the inference. That her father—a tough army boot-camp instructor—had been vehement in his opposition to her being involved with anyone in the military. After Mrs. Spencer's words, he now wondered if it was because Jessi's dad and the entire base had witnessed the hell his mom had gone through because of his dad. Because of the way he'd used the bottle to blot out the demons related to his war deployment. It hadn't worked. He'd just created a living hell for everyone around him. Clint wouldn't want any daughter of his to go through what his mom had on a daily basis.

Whatever Mr. Spencer's reasons, it had ended up saving Clint's hide down at that creek. It—and his enlistment papers—had given him the perfect out for leaving Richmond. He'd jumped at the excuse, although he now realized that's all it had been. An excuse. He'd been afraid *of* his dad and *for* his dad. Had run away from the possibility that he might turn out to be just like him. But most of all, he hadn't wanted anyone to know the shame he'd felt.

The irony was, they had known, according to Abigail.

"No," Jessi said. "I wouldn't have shared my secrets with just anyone."

The hint of accusation in her voice was unmistakable. Because she had shared *her* secret with someone: him. But he hadn't returned the favor by telling her his. Maybe because he hadn't wanted to add any more to her plate. Maybe because the only thing he'd wanted at the time had been to erase the pain in her eyes.

Instead, he'd ended up making love to her and adding to his long list of sins. Which included leaving her the very next day. He'd thought it was to protect her.

Not that it had done any good. Jessi's own daughter was now struggling with trauma related to her military service, so he hadn't ended up protecting her from anything. Just his own ugly past and uncertain future.

Little had she known back then that he had harbored a secret crush on her. Maybe it had been part of the whole badass, wanting-to-redeem-himself syndrome. The same reason he'd enlisted. A need to redeem himself and maybe even his father—or at least to make peace with what had happened.

Clint's job, though, had turned into a passion he just couldn't shake. In some small measure he *had* redeemed himself. Each time he was able to help an emotionally wounded soldier have a shot at a normal life, he was some-how giving his father the help he'd never received when he'd been alive. And in doing that—Clint flexed his damaged finger again—he helped protect their sons and daughters.

Abigail broke into his thoughts. "I really am sorry. I just assumed that Jessi knew, since you went to school together."

They'd done more than just that. Which was something he could not—would not—think about right now. Not with her mom sitting there, looking more than a little mortified.

"It's fine…"

"Don't worry…"

He and Jessi spoke at exactly the same time, which caused everyone to laugh and broke the tension instantly. Even Cooper gave a quick *woof* of approval.

And although he'd been the one to say, "Don't worry," he was worried. More than a little. Because every time he caught Jessi watching him, his gut slid sideways.

"I have some peach ice cream for dessert," Abigail said, "if anyone wants some."

He glanced down at his watch. Almost nine. He could safely take off and claim to have survived the evening. "Thank you, but I probably should be heading home. I have an early morning tomorrow."

He pushed his chair back, dislodging Cooper from his foot in the process. The dog's nails clicked on the hard-wood floor as he slid from beneath the table and pressed his cheek against Clint's calf. Reaching down, he scratched behind the animal's ears.

"Are you sure?" Abigail asked.

"Yes, unless there's something I can do to help clean up."

She smiled. "Not a thing." A quick frown puckered her brow. "I almost forgot. When can I see Chelsea? I don't want to set her treatment back, but if I can just spend a minute or two with her to assure myself that she's really—"

"Of course." He glanced at Jessi for confirmation. "How about if we make it for the next time Jessi and I meet with her? Friday at three?"

Jessi nodded her approval. "It's okay with me. I want to talk to you a little bit about her condition first, though, okay, Mama? I don't want you to be shocked by what she might say…or not say."

"I wasn't born yesterday. I know it's bad. I just want to see her."

"I'll pick you up on my way home from work, then. We can go together." She kissed her mother on the cheek, something that made Clint's chest tighten. Despite Mr. Spencer's heavy-handed ways, this had been a house of love. It was obvious the two women were close. And he was glad. Glad that her teenage angst hadn't left any lasting scars.

His arthritic pinky creaked out a warning shot when he curled his hand around the chair to push it back in.

"Thanks again for dinner, Mrs. Spencer."

"You're very welcome, and I'm glad you came. I already feel better."

As he started for the door, he was surprised to find Jessi right behind him. "I'll walk you to your car."

He opened the door, forgetting about Cooper. The dog bounded out before he could stop him.

"It's okay," Jessi said. "He does it to everyone. He won't go far."

The walk down the driveway was filled with the scent of magnolia blossoms, a smell he remembered well. Unbeknownst to Jessi, he'd sat in front of her house for hours the night of graduation, listening for any sounds of fighting, or worse. It had been hard back then to remember that not every father struck out with his fists.

But there'd been nothing that night. Just the muggy heat and that rich floral scent—something he connected to Jessi every time he smelled it. Even now, memories of the soft carpet of moss he'd felt beneath his hands as he'd supported his weight swirled around him. Of her face, soft and flushed, tilting back as he'd trailed his mouth down her neck.

Damn. He never should have come here.

He quickened his steps, only to have her hand touch his arm as they reached his car. He turned to face her, keys in hand, ready to get the hell out of there. The faster he left, the sooner he could regain his sanity.

Which right now was nowhere to be found. Because all he wanted to do was kiss her. Right in front of her house. To relive a little of the magic he'd experienced all those years ago.

"Why didn't you tell me…back then?" she asked.

He might have known this was why she'd wanted to come with him. "I thought I'd explained that. It was my problem, there was no reason to involve anyone else."

"God, Clint. I bawled my eyes out about my dad's stupid rules without even knowing what you—"

"I didn't tell you because I didn't want anyone to know. Besides, it doesn't matter anymore. It's all in the past."

"And your dad is gone."

His jaw clenched. His father's liver cancer, brought on by years of alcohol abuse, didn't mitigate the fact that Clint wished he'd known sooner how to help him. "So is yours."

"Yes. I'm just glad he's not suffering. The strokes came faster at the end…"

"I'm sorry." He put his arm around her, meaning to give her a quick squeeze and release her. Instead, somehow she wound up against his chest, palms splayed against his shirt, staring up at him with those huge eyes.

The same eyes that did something to his insides every damn time she looked at him. It had happened in high school. And it was still happening now. He leaned back against the car door, still holding on to her.

She bit her lip for a second. "For what it's worth, I'm glad you were the one—back then. And I'm glad it's you now."

Whoa. If that wasn't a kick in the gut, he didn't know what was. She was glad he'd been the one who'd taken her virginity and not Larry? He'd beaten himself up about that for years afterwards.

And what did she mean, she was happy it was him now? She had to be talking about Chelsea.

"I had no idea who she was, Jess, until you stepped into that room. I swear."

"I didn't know it was you either. Until I saw the name-plate on your desk."

Her fingers came up and touched the line of his jaw, and she smiled. "I never believed that rebel freedom air you put on back in school."

He cocked a brow. "Oh, no? And why was that?"

"Because you looked so lost at times. I just never understood what caused it back then."

Before he had time to tense up, she continued. "Mama is right, you know."

"How's that?"

"You are the absolute best person to be treating Chelsea." She closed her eyes for a second before looking up at him again. "I'm so glad you're here, Clint. So glad you came home."

The squeezing sensation in his chest grew. The tight-rope he was toeing his way across was thinner than he'd realized...harder to balance on than he'd expected.

"Promise me you won't drop the case," she added.

That's exactly what he *should* do. Especially now. Bow out and ask someone else to step in. Transfer the hell out of that hospital and go back to California.

A thought came to him. Was this why Jessi was in his arms, staring all doe-eyed at him? "I can't make you that promise. I have to do what I think is in the best interests of your daughter."

"I know. Just promise me that tomorrow, when you walk into that office, you'll still be the one treating her."

He was suddenly aware of her fingers. They were still on his skin, only now they'd moved slightly backward, putting his senses on high alert—along with certain parts of his body. "I'll be there for her."

"Good. Because I think I'm about to do something very, very stupid."

He didn't need to ask what it was. Because he was on the verge of doing something just as stupid.

But it didn't stop him from tugging her closer, neither did it stop his lips from closing over hers in a sudden crazy burst of need.

And once their mouths fused together, he was transported to the past. Twenty-two years, to be exact. He'd been unable to get enough of her. Her taste. The faint scent of her shampoo or body wash, or magnolias—whatever the hell it had been that had filled his senses, intoxicating him more than the booze he'd been offered earlier ever could have.

A faint sound came from her throat. He was fairly certain it wasn't a gasp of protest, since her arms had wound around his neck and her body had slid up his as she'd gone up on tiptoe. He buried his fingers in the hair at her nape, the slight dampness probably due to the Virginia humidity, but it brought back memories of perspiration and bodies that moved together in perfect harmony. Of…

The sound of Cooper's plaintive howl split the air a short distance away, followed by the sound of the front door opening. Abigail's voice called out the dog's name.

Cursing everything under the sun, he let Jessi pull free from his lips, even though the last thing he wanted to do was let her go. He wanted to drag her into the car and drive right to the creek to see if that night had been everything he'd remembered it being.

Abigail's voice called the dog's name again. The bushes shielded them from view, so Clint didn't look. Besides, his gaze was glued to Jessi's pale features.

Even when Cooper decided to lumber over to them, instead of going to the house, he didn't break eye contact.

"Sorry. I'm sorry." The gutted apology as she backed up one step, then two, made his lungs burn. The back of her hand went to her mouth, and she pressed hard. Her feet separated them by another pace, then she reached down to capture Cooper's collar. "Please, don't dump her. This was my fault. Not hers."

As she led the dog back to the front door, Clint gave his head a silent shake. There was no one else. He couldn't leave. Not yet.

Chelsea couldn't afford to lose two doctors in the space of two weeks.

Which meant Clint couldn't afford to start something he would never be able to finish. He'd made love to Jessi once and had barely been able to find the strength to walk away. If it happened twice, there was no hope for him.

So, from now on, he would tread carefully. And keep his distance from Jessi and her mom as much as possible.

CHAPTER SEVEN

CHELSEA WAS TALKING.

Not a lot, but Clint had noticed a subtle shift in her demeanor over the past several days as they met for their sessions. She was more interested and less withdrawn. He wasn't sure what had caused the change, but he was all for it.

Besides, it kept him from having to deal with the devastating consequences of that kiss he and Jessi had shared beside his car. And the suspicious thoughts that had crept into his mind in the meantime.

Had she tried to manipulate him into staying?

No. Jessi wasn't like that. When he'd left all those years ago, she'd never said a word to try to make him change his mind. Yes, she'd made him promise that he'd remain on her daughter's case—right before she'd locked her lips to his, but it wasn't as if she was the only one who'd been thinking along those lines. He'd been just as guilty. And she'd been very careful to maintain her distance ever since. Their consultations were now over the phone—despite their earlier agreement to meet with Chelsea together—and her voice during those calls was brisk and businesslike.

Just like the doctor she was.

And she was smart. She knew exactly the right questions to ask regarding her daughter's state of mind. According to the nurses, her visits to Chelsea occurred during his off hours. He had no doubt she'd somehow found out his schedule and was purposely coming when he wasn't around.

As grateful as he should be for the breathing space, he found himself irritated at the way he missed her presence.

What else could he do, though? He'd always prided himself on his self-control, because it was something his dad had never had much of. And yet Clint lost it every time he was around Jessi.

Every. Damn. Time.

It had been true twenty-two years ago, and it was still true today. He just couldn't resist her. The good girl that he'd had a secret crush on in high school had turned him into an impulsive, reckless creature. One he feared, because he recognized the beast all too well. He'd looked into impulsive, reckless eyes so like his own during his teenage years.

That raw, angry kid had morphed into a cool, rational man somewhere along the way, and in doing so had found himself. Had found an antidote that worked. But it only functioned if he didn't let anyone get too close.

Today would be the test. Jessi was due here with her mom in a little over an hour. He'd warned himself. Scolded himself. Immersed himself in work. All to no avail.

His heart was already pounding in anticipation of seeing her—trying to justify being with her one more time.

Just one kiss. He could stop anytime he wanted.

Sound familiar, Clint?

Substitute *drink* for the word *kiss* and you had his dad in all his lying glory.

Not good.

His assistant pushed open the door. "Dr. Marks? Miles Branson is here for his appointment. Are you ready for him?"

"Yes, send him in. Thanks, Maria."

As hectic as his morning had been, with two new patients and a flurry of consultations, he shouldn't have had time to think about Jessi at all. But she'd found her way into every nook and cranny of his brain and surged to the forefront whenever he had a free moment.

Like now.

Miles came in and, after shaking Clint's hand, lowered himself into one of the chairs across from him. Another PTSD patient, this particular man had made great strides in his treatment over the past couple of weeks. It could be because of that new baby girl he had waiting at home for him.

"How're Maggie and the baby?" he asked.

"Both beautiful." The smile the man gave him was genuine, and the furrows between his brows seemed less pronounced than they'd been when Clint had arrived. He scrolled through his phone for a second and then handed it over.

Miles's wife and a baby swaddled in a pink blanket lay on a hospital bed. She looked exhausted but happy, while it was obvious their daughter was trying out her new set of lungs, if the open mouth and red, angry-looking face were anything to go by.

"Beautiful. You've got a great pair of girls there." Clint pushed the phone across his desk.

"I'm a lucky man." He smiled again, glancing down at his wife and daughter. "You know, for the first time in a long time I actually believe that."

"I know you do. Are you ready to try for a reduction of your medication?"

"Can I do away with it altogether?"

Clint paused for a second. While his superiors were very conscious of time and money, his only concern was for his patients. He'd been known to ruffle a few feathers along the way, but had still somehow made it up the chain of command. While paroxetine wasn't addictive, like the benzodiazepine family of medications, he still felt it was safer to reduce the dosage gradually while maintaining a regular therapy schedule as they progressed.

In the two years since Miles had first been seen by other doctors, the man had gotten engaged and then married to a wonderful woman who knew exactly what he was battling. And, thank heavens, this man hadn't shown the agitation and anger issues that Clint's dad had.

"Let's knock it down from sixty milligrams a day to twenty and go from there." He grabbed his prescription pad and wrote out a new dosage recommendation. "We'll maintain our sessions, and in a couple of weeks, if all goes well, we'll reduce them even more. How does that sound?"

Miles sat back in his chair, his posture relaxed and open. "It sounds like living. Thanks, Doc."

For the next forty-five minutes they went through the new father's moods and actions, detailing where he'd struggled, while Clint made notes he would transcribe later. Together they made a plan on how to deal with the next several weeks, when having a new baby at home would put more stress on both him and the family.

When they finally parted, he opened the office door to let Miles out and his glance immediately connected with Jessi and her mom, who'd arrived fifteen minutes early for their session with Chelsea. He nodded at the pair, walking Miles over to his assistant's desk and giving a few last-minute instructions on scheduling.

Taking a deep breath, he finally turned and made his way over to the pair in his waiting area. Jessi, dressed in a casual white-flowered dress that stretched snugly across her top and waist, stood to her feet. Flat, strappy sandals showed off pink toenails and dainty feet. He swallowed when he realized he'd been staring. All his misgivings from earlier came roaring back. He shoved them aside.

"Sorry to keep you waiting," he muttered, his voice a little gruffer than he'd expected. But seeing Jessi up close and personal created this choking sensation that closed off the upper part of his throat.

Her mom was the one to break the stare-fest. "We were a little early, at my insistence. I'm anxious to see my grand-daughter."

"I'm sure you are."

Abigail was in a pair of jeans with a white button-down shirt. At almost sixty, she was still a beautiful woman, with high cheekbones and eyes very like her daughter's. And her granddaughter's, for that matter.

"Do you want to meet in my office or head down to Chelsea's room? Jessi gave a little shrug, no longer attempting to look directly at him. Maybe she felt as un-comfortable as he was about this meeting. "Wherever you feel is best."

Her mom spoke up again. "I haven't seen Chelsea's room. Do you think she would mind if we met her there? I'm curious about where she's been staying." She blinked a couple of times. "Not that I'm saying there's anything wrong with the hospital. It looks modern and well cared for."

Not what she'd expected. She didn't say the words, but he could imagine her thoughts.

The VA's reputation had taken a beating in the press over the last year. And not without reason, but the corruption was slowly being weeded out, and Clint hoped the end result would be a system of hospitals the country's service-men and women could be proud of.

Clint had done his best to make sure his patients received the best treatment possible. And he knew there were a lot of other dedicated doctors who also cared deeply about their patients. The waiting lists were staggering, and, yes, it would probably be much easier to find work in the civilian sector for better pay and a lighter workload. But that wasn't why he did what he did.

"You're fine," he assured Abigail. He turned to his assistant. "Could you call down to Chelsea's room and let her know we're on our way?"

"Of course, Doctor." She picked up her phone and dialed as Clint nodded toward the hallway to their right. "Jessi, you know the way."

She stood and slung the strap of her purse over her arm, making sure her mother was following her. She glanced back at him. "Any last-minute instructions?"

"No. Chelsea's been more open, as I told you over the phone. I think that's an encouraging sign." Not that they'd made definitive steps in her treatment. The new class of antidepressants he'd prescribed was kicking in, though, so he had hopes that as the fog of despair continued to lift, she would start looking to the future, instead of crouching in the past. They had yet to talk about the specifics surrounding her months in captivity. She'd reiterated that she hadn't been tortured or assaulted, but as to what exactly had happened during that time, there was still a large swath of information that was missing. Clint had even tried going through channels and seeing if her superior officers knew anything more. But they were what Clint would label as "careful" with their words. It hadn't been anything in particular that was or wasn't said. It had just been the way the information had been delivered. And every story had been told in an identical fashion.

For Clint, that fact alone raised a huge red flag.

"Nana!" he heard the greeting even before he reached the room. And the happiness in that one word was apparent. As was the sight of the two women embracing, while Jessi stood back to allow the reunion to happen.

"How's she really doing?" she asked him in a low voice

as Abigail sat on the edge of the bed, her arm around her granddaughter.

"Just like I said. She's talking more."

"Any idea yet on the why?"

The why of the suicide attempt.

"We haven't made it that far, yet."

The exchange ended when Abigail waved her daughter over. "Doesn't she look wonderful?"

She didn't, and they all knew it. Still pale and frighteningly thin, Chelsea did not have the appearance of a soldier who'd been through the worst that boot camp had to offer… who had survived a stint as a POW. She looked like a fragile piece of china that might shatter at the slightest tap.

While they talked, Clint grabbed two chairs from an empty room that adjoined Chelsea's and added them to the two that were already against the pale gray walls—Clint had learned how important equalizing the setting was, which was why his office had three identical chairs. One for him and two for those who met him there. His rank was above that of many of his patients, but that didn't mean he had to act the part.

"Dr. Marks?" Jessi's voice interrupted his thoughts.

Although it rankled at some level, he knew it was better for them to address each other in a formal manner in public, although he'd told Chelsea—in vague terms—that he and Jessi had known each other in the past. It was easier to be as truthful as possible, while holding back information that could be deemed harmful to her treatment.

"Sorry," he murmured. He turned to Chelsea. "Do you feel up to sitting with us?"

"Yes." She swung her legs over the side of the bed, waving off her mom, who'd immediately moved to help her. "It's okay. I can do it."

She was in a set of flannel pajamas that Jessi had evidently brought in during one of her other visits. Ideally, he would have liked her to be dressed in normal clothes for their meetings. And in recent days she'd made more of an effort.

So why was today different?

Was she trying to appear fragile, warning away any talk that crept toward painful subjects?

It was too late now to ask her to change, and he didn't want to do anything that would upset Jessi's mom in the process. Besides, he had another client in an hour and a half and he wanted to make sure that Chelsea wouldn't be cut off in the middle of anything important.

They sat in a circle. Chelsea and Abigail glanced at him expectantly, while Jessi's gaze was centered on the folded hands she held in her lap.

"Chelsea, it's been a while since your grandmother has seen you, am I correct?"

The young woman's hand snaked out and grabbed Abigail's. "I'm glad she's here."

"So am I."

He wasn't going to push hard this session, he just wanted to reintroduce the family and make sure everyone knew that their old ways of interacting might not work in this new and different world. Chelsea had gone to war as one person and had come back another. They all had yet to see where exactly that left her mom and grandmother, although the reunion had gone much more smoothly than he would have expected.

Even as he thought it, Abigail pressed her fingertips to her eyes and wiped away moisture that had gathered beneath them. "Oh, no, Nana. Don't cry." Chelsea wrapped her arms around the older woman. "Mom, there's a box of tissues in my top drawer. Would you mind getting me one?"

Jessi jumped up and headed toward the small end table beside the bed. She drew out the top drawer, found the box and withdrew it. Then she stopped. Chelsea was facing away from her mother and couldn't see her, but Clint could. A strange look crossed her face as she peered at something inside that drawer. She started to reach for it then withdrew her hand.

Chelsea, as if realizing something was wrong, swiveled around in her chair. "Can't you find…? Oh, no, Mom. Please don't."

But it was already too late, because Jessi had reached back into the drawer and withdrawn what looked like a wad of tissues. Glancing at Chelsea and seeing the horror in her eyes, he realized that's not what that was. Not at all.

Even as he looked, Jess smoothed down the bottom edge of the thin paper and came forward a couple of steps, only to stop halfway. It was a doll of some sort.

No. Not a doll. A baby. Painstakingly crafted from the tissues in the box in her drawer.

"Chelsea, honey." Jessi's voice dropped away for a second before coming back again. "What is this?"

CHAPTER EIGHT

JESSI SLUMPED IN a chair in Clint's office. "I don't understand. What could it mean?"

Her daughter had refused to talk about the strange item, withdrawing back into her shell until Clint called a halt to the session and let Chelsea crawl back into her bed. She'd silently held out her hand for the doll and laid it carefully back inside the drawer.

The act made Jessi shiver.

She'd sent her mom home with a promise to stop by later, and Clint had ordered the nurse to call him immediately if there was any change.

"I don't know what it means. Maybe she miscarried while she was overseas. Maybe it's something she made as a coping mechanism. There could be any number of explanations, but until she tells us we won't know for sure."

"Will you ask her again tomorrow?"

"I'll see how she is. We may have to work our way toward it slowly." He dragged his fingers through his hair and leaned back in his chair. "It could just be a dead end."

"Who makes a doll out of a box of tissues? It just doesn't seem…normal."

When he stared at her, she closed her eyes. "Sorry. That didn't come out right. It's just that everything seemed to explode out of nowhere two months ago."

"I know. It just takes time."

"What if she never gets better? What if she's like this for the rest of her life?"

He reached across and covered her hand with his. "Thoughts like that aren't going to help anyone."

"Did you struggle with those kinds of thoughts during high school? About your dad? Did *he* ever get better?"

When he went to withdraw his hand with a frown, she grabbed at his fingers, holding him in place.

"Oh, God, Clint, I'm so sorry," she whispered. "I'm just worried about Chelsea."

"I know." He laced his fingers through hers. "I gave her a sedative, so she should sleep through the night. We'll start fresh in the morning."

"I want to be there when she wakes up."

He studied her for a minute or two, before shaking his head with what looked like regret. "I don't think that's a good idea, Jess. When you and your mom left, she was agitated and withdrawn. I don't want those memories to be the ones that resurface when she opens her eyes. Give her a day."

"A day?" She couldn't believe he was asking her to stay away from the hospital for an entire day. "I'm not the only one worried. Mom is, as well."

"I'll call you as soon as I see her. Are you working tomorrow?" He let go of her hand and reached for one of his pencils, jiggling it between his fingers as if he needed something to keep him busy. Or maybe it was a hint that he needed to get back to work.

"I'm on the afternoon shift, starting at three. I'd better get out of your hair." She stood to her feet, then thought of something. "What if you get a call in the middle of the night?"

"If something serious happens, I'll be in touch."

"Promise?"

"Promise." He must have read her dubious smile, because one side of his mouth curved into that familiar half smile. "Would you like me to pinkie-swear, as well?"

Despite her worry, she found her own lips twitching. "Would you, if I asked you to?"

"Yes."

Something icy hot nipped the air between them. She held her breath and then released it in a long stream. "Or you could come and spend the night at the house. Just in case."

Why on earth had she asked that? It was too late to take back the offer, although she could clarify it. "On the couch, of course."

His eyes softened, but he shook his head. "I have to work for a couple more hours. Besides, I don't think my staying with you would be a good idea, Jess. Things never quite remain that simple between us. And I meant what I said about taking myself off the case if I think my objectivity has been compromised."

Oh, Lord, that's right. He'd intimated that he'd hand Chelsea over to someone else if things got too personal between them. "I wasn't asking you to sleep with me. Not this time."

She'd gone that route once before, asking him to make love to her by the creek, desperately needing a few minutes out from beneath her father's thumb.

"I don't remember complaining the last time you did."

No. But then again she hadn't seen him volunteering to hang around the next day—although it had probably been too late for him to back out of boot camp by that time. And who was to say he would stick around in Richmond now? Some servicemen loved the adventure of a new place every couple of years. Not Jessi. Once she'd gotten to high school, her father had finally seemed willing to settle down and stay until she graduated. Then she'd married Larry, who hadn't known she'd had a dalliance with his friend. Not until that last day of his life.

She blocked out the thought and concentrated on the here and now as Clint got up and opened the door to his office.

She walked through it and then hesitated on the other side. "So you'll call me tomorrow."

"As soon as I have some news. Yes."

They said their goodbyes, and already his manner was more aloof. Businesslike.

Once she got to the front door of the hospital she lifted her chin and made a decision. If Clint could keep his personal life separate from what happened at the hospital, then she could, too. For everyone's sakes, she was going to have to learn to take her cues from Clint, adopting that same professional demeanor whenever she was here.

No matter how hard it was starting to be.

The suicide had come out of nowhere, and while it hadn't been one of Clint's patients it brought home the thin line he was walking with Chelsea and Jessi. The entire hospital was on edge because of it.

It wasn't easy for any doctor to lose a patient, no matter what anyone said. True impartiality was hard to come by at the best of times...and with Jessi it seemed to border on the impossible.

He'd felt the anguish radiating from every pore of her body when she'd lifted that macabre paper figure out of her daughter's drawer. And it had taken a lot of self-restraint to remain in his seat, observing Chelsea's reactions, and not rush over to make sure the woman who wasn't his patient was okay.

While he and Jessi hadn't been involved emotionally in the past—a thought he stubbornly clung to, no matter what his gut said—there could be nothing at all between them now.

Not just because of his patient. Not just because of his and Jessi's past. But because of his job and his own personal baggage.

Once they found a replacement for him, he was headed back to San Diego. It was either that or request that his transfer to Richmond be made permanent, something he couldn't see happening. He was the one they called on for temporary assignments. It's what he wanted. Moving around a lot kept his mind on the job at hand, rather than highlighting his lack of a personal life. And the unlikelihood that he'd ever have much of one.

Not that he hadn't tried. He'd been in serious relationships. Twice. But both times the woman had left, saying she felt he was withholding himself emotionally.

He had been. Somehow he could never quite let his guard all the way down. His every move was calculated. Controlled. And that's the way he liked it.

He was very aware that wasn't what most women looked for in a man. He was just not husband material.

Because of his dad?

Hell, the second Jessi had mentioned his father in his office he'd tried to yank his hand away, very aware that his crooked finger was right there for her to see. And ask about. The last thing he wanted to talk about was his past. Jessi's father might have been a pain-in-the-ass drill sergeant—but at least he'd loved her enough to care about who she saw. What she did.

His cell phone beeped. When he glanced at the caller ID, he winced. Jessi. The very person presently haunting his every thought. And it was already midmorning. He was supposed to have called her to let her know how Chelsea was.

He pressed the answer button and bit out an apology.

"Sorry, Jess. We've been swamped and I hadn't had a chance to call you yet."

She brushed aside his apology with a cleared throat. "Was she okay when she woke up?"

Despite the worry in her tone, her voice flowed over him, soothing away some of the worst parts of his morning. A few muscles in his jaw relaxed.

"I haven't had an in-depth conversation with her. Just a few minutes of small talk as she ate breakfast. We're due to have a therapy session at two."

"But she's okay."

He realized what she was looking for, and all the day's heartache came roaring back. "She doesn't seem to be obsessing over what happened yesterday. I'll call you when I've talked to her again."

"Hmm." She didn't say anything more.

"I know I promised. I'm sorry." He gritted his teeth.

"No, it's just that I have to be at work at three, and I'll probably be just as swamped with patients as you seem to be, since it's a holiday."

Ah, yes. Father's Day. Something he tried to forget every year. He glanced down at his left hand, where the crook in his finger reminded him of a whole childhood of fear and unhappiness. That wasn't the only reason he wasn't crazy about this particular day. At this point in his life, he didn't see himself ever carrying the title of father, even if he found someone and married her. He was close to forty, and had never really given kids much of a thought.

Maybe he should ask Jessi if the day held any special significance for Chelsea, though…good or bad. He should be prepared for any eventuality.

"Will Father's Day add to Chelsea's stress levels?"

There was silence over the line for a long minute. "No. Larry died before she was born. She only knows him through pictures." There was something sad about the way she said it.

He forced the next words out even as his insides tightened. "You didn't have much time together."

"No, we didn't. The worst thing is he might still be alive if someone hadn't…" The words ended on a strangled note.

Something burned in his gut. "If someone hadn't what, Jess?

"It doesn't matter. What does is that I have a wonderful daughter from our union. That's what made the hard times after his death bearable."

The image of Jessi mourning her husband was enough to make that burning sensation tickle the back of his throat. She'd had a daughter with the man. And as much as he told himself he didn't care, the cold reality was that part of him did—the same part that had leaped when he'd first realized who Jessi was and had wondered if Chelsea might be his.

But she wasn't. And if he was going to do his job, he had to remember that and keep on remembering it.

"About my session with her. How about if I send you a text, rather than trying to call? That way you can check in when you've got a free moment."

"That would be fantastic. Thank you, Clint. But please do call if something changes. I'll set my ringer to vibrate just for your number. If it does, I'll know it's important, and I'll find a way to answer, or I'll call you right back."

The tension in his gut eased and something warm and dangerous took its place. She was going to be listening for his call and his call only.

Okay, idiot. It's in case of an emergency. It's not like she's putting your number on speed dial or anything.

"So you have the number here, if you have any questions or need something, right? I remember you said my card was on your refrigerator." He glanced at the business card on his desk, since he hadn't quite memorized his Richmond number yet. "Or do you need me to read it off to you again?"

"Nope. I've already programmed it into my phone. In fact, I have you on speed dial," she said. "Just in case."

CHAPTER NINE

FATHER'S DAY SHOULD be outlawed.

Or at least the giving of gifts involving any type of motor should be banned. So far that afternoon, Jessi had treated a leg that been kissed by a chain saw, a back injury from an ATV accident and a lawn mower that had collided with a lamppost before bouncing back and knocking its new owner unconscious. Not to mention assorted other minor injuries. And she still had two hours to go until the end of her shift. The one thing she hadn't seen had been the screen on her cell phone lighting up or feeling its vibration coming from the pocket of her scrubs.

All was silent with Clint and her daughter.

Sighing, she grabbed the next chart and headed for the curtained exam room. Patient name: William Tuppele. Complaint: the words *fishing hook* and *earlobe* ran through her head before she blinked and forced her eyes to read back over that part.

Okay. So it wasn't just things with motors that should be banned from this particular holiday.

When she entered the room, a man dressed in hip waders with a camo T-shirt tucked into them sat on the exam table. And, yep, he was sporting a shiny new piece of jewelry.

She looked closer and gulped. Had something behind his ear just moved?

Stepping farther in the room, she glanced again at his chart. "Mr. Tuppele." She omitted the words *How are you?* because it was pretty obvious this was the last place the man wanted to be. Instead, she aimed for cheeky. "Catch anything interesting today?"

Instead of smiling, the man scowled. "Great, I get a nurse who thinks she's a comedienne."

She bristled, but held out her hand anyway. "I'm Dr. Riley. How long have you been like this?"

"About an hour." His gaze skipped away from hers, his words slurring the slightest bit. "My son caught me with his hook. It was his first fishing trip."

"Hmm." She kept the sound as noncommittal as possible, but from the way his face had turned scarlet and—she tried not to fan herself openly—the alcohol fumes that bathed every word the man spoke, she would almost bet there was no "son" involved in this particular party. Rather, she suspected a male-bonding episode that had gone terribly wrong.

Hip waders and booze. Not a good combination. They were lucky no one had drowned. "Did someone drive you to the hospital?"

She certainly didn't want to let a drunk loose on the roads.

"One of my buddies. He's down in the waiting room."

Jessi could only hope the *buddy* had been less generous when it came to doling out those cans of beer to himself. She made a mental note to have someone check on his friend's sobriety level.

She sat on her stool just as the worm—and, yes, it was indeed a piece of live bait—gave a couple of frantic wiggles. Lord, she did not want to touch that thing, much less have to handle it. But the best way to remove a fishing hook was to cut off the end opposite the barb and push the shank on through, rather than risk more damage by pulling it back out the way it had gone in. That barb acted like a one-way door. They went in, but they didn't want to come out.

The worm moved again.

"Hell," said the man. "Can you please get this damned thing off me? It stinks."

And it's creeping me out.

Mr. Tuppele didn't say the words, but she could well imagine him thinking them, because the same thoughts were circling around in her head, too. Maybe this was the worm's way of exacting revenge on anglers everywhere.

And maybe she could call one of the male nurses.

Ha! And give her patient a reason for his earlier sexist remark. Hardly. "When was your last tetanus shot?"

"Haven't been to a doctor in twenty years. Wouldn't be here now if one of my...er, my son hadn't been so squeamish about taking it out himself. "Is my ear going to be permanently pierced? I don't cotton to men with earrings and such."

She smiled despite herself, tempted to match his it-was-my-son fib and tell him that, yes, he would be permanently disfigured and might as well go out and buy a couple of nice dangly pieces of jewelry. But she restrained herself. "No. I knew a man who had his ear pierced in high school but had to stop wearing an earring when he went into the military. It's all healed up now."

At least she assumed that's when Clint had stopped wearing the single hoop in his ear, because there was no sign of it now. And how was it that she had even noticed that? Or remembered what he'd worn back then?

She'd kind of liked his earring, back in the day.

"Good. Don't need anyone getting any strange ideas about me."

Too late for that, Mr. Tuppele. She already had a few ideas about him. And they went much deeper than men sporting earrings. "Let me set up. I'm going to call in a nurse to give you a shot to numb your ear."

"I don't need it numbed. I just need that damned thing out."

"Are you sure?" The rest of the staff was going to thank her patient for sparing them the need to get close to that wriggler.

"Just do it."

"Okay." Trying not to shudder, she got her equipment together, praying the worm died before she had to deal with it. As disgusting as she found it, she felt a twinge of pity for the creature. It hadn't been its choice to be cast into a river for the first hungry fish to gulp.

Gloves in place, she squirted some alcohol on the wound in back of his ear, waiting for the string of cuss words to die down before continuing. She grabbed her locking forceps and clamped the instrument right behind the worm. If the barb had gone all the way through his ear, she could have just cut it off and backed the hook out, worm and all. But while there was a tiny bit of metal showing in the front of the lobe, the barb was still embedded in the man's flesh. It was going to hurt, pushing it the rest of the way through. She got a pair of wire cutters and took a deep breath, then moved in and cut the eye, leaving as much shank as possible behind that worm.

"Okay, I'm going to have to push the barb through the front, are you sure you're okay?"

"Fine."

Holding the front of the man's earlobe with her gloved fingers, she used the forceps to push hard, until the barb popped through.

The man yelled out a few more choice words, but he'd

held remarkably steady. Having a hook shoved through your ear was evidently a surefire way to sober up. Fast.

"All right, the worst part is over. I just need to pull the hook the rest of the way out." Holding a tray beneath his ear so she wouldn't have to touch the worm, she removed the forceps and used them to grasp the barb in front. Then she pulled steadily, until the worm plonked onto the instrument tray and the hook was the rest of the way through his ear.

Praying the creature didn't find his way off the counter and onto the floor, she set the tray down and used a piece of antiseptic soaked gauze to sponge away the blood and dirt from the front and the back of the man's ear and then took a piece of dry gauze and applied pressure to stop the bleeding. "Can you hold this here? We'll need to get you a tetanus shot as well as some antibiotics, just in case."

Mr. Tuppele did as she asked and squeezed his earlobe between the two sides of gauze. But when she carried the worm over to the garbage can, the man stopped her with a yelled "Hey!"

She turned toward him, still holding the tray. "Yes?"

"That thing dead?"

She glanced down. It wasn't moving any more, thank God. "I think so."

"Touch it to make sure."

Horror filled her to the core. She hated fishing. Hated bugs. Broken bones, bullet wounds, she could whiz through with ease, but anything that wiggled or crawled or stared with cold-blooded eyes she was just not into. "I'll let you do the honors." She held out the tray and let the man jab the worm with a finger while she cringed. Thankfully it remained limp, even after two more pokes.

"Damn. I was hoping to use that one again."

Again? Hooking himself once hadn't been enough?

She gave a mental eye roll. "Sorry about that. It was probably the alcohol."

"There ain't that much in my blood."

And... Okay.

Dumping the worm and the cleaning gauze into the trash bin, she turned back to face him. "I'll have the nurse come in with the shot and your prescription. Make sure you see your doctor if that ear puffs up or doesn't seem to be healing after a couple of days. Or if you develop a fever."

She took the gauze from him and checked his ear, before pressing tiny round bandages over the front and back of the puncture wound. "You can take those off in a couple of hours."

The man managed to mumble out a "Thank you."

Her phone buzzed, making her jump.

Clint. It had to be.

Patting the man on the back and telling him to take care, she went out and gave instructions to the nurse and asked her to send someone out to check on his buddy. By that time her phone had stopped ringing. "Anyone else waiting for me?"

The nurse grinned. "Not at the moment. But the new barbecue grills are probably being fired up even as we speak."

"Heaven help us all."

Hopefully, that wave of patients would come through after she was off duty. She forced out a laugh, even though she was dying to grab her phone and call Clint back. He knew she was on duty. Knew she'd get back to him as soon as she could.

The nurse got the injection ready and carried it into the room, leaving Jessi alone in the hallway. She took out her phone and glanced at the readout, even though she knew who it was.

C. Marks.

Hitting the redial button, she leaned a shoulder against the wall, an ache settling in her back at all the bending she'd done today.

"Marks here."

"Clint? It's Jessi. What's up?"

"Just calling to see how much longer you were on duty."

Jessi glanced at her watch. "I have another half hour, why?"

"I thought we might get together and talk about Chelsea."

"Is something wrong?"

"No, she's fine. No major developments, but no setbacks either. I just haven't eaten, and I assume you haven't either. Would you like to go somewhere? Or I could come to the hospital and eat with you in the cafeteria."

She grimaced, glancing at the room she'd just come from. "No. The food here isn't the best, and I'm not really hungry. I could do with a shake, though, while you get something else."

She was still puzzling over his sudden change of heart.

"A shake sounds fine. How about we get it to go?"

Okay, she hadn't thought this far ahead. "And go where?"

"We could go to the park on the east side."

The park? She glanced out at the streetlights that were already visible in the darkening sky. "Sounds like a plan."

"Good. I'll meet you at the front entrance of the hospital, okay?"

"I'll be there."

Maybe somehow in that period of time she could shake off all thoughts of sitting inside Clint's car in a dark park, sipping on a milk shake. Or the fleeting images of what they could do once they finished their drinks and had said all they needed to say.

A warning came up from the depths of her soul, reminding her of days gone by and how badly he'd broken her heart. But only because she'd let him.

You can't head down that road again, Jess.

No, she couldn't.

Well, if her heart could make that decree, then she could somehow abide by it.

So she would have to make one thing very clear to herself before he came to pick her up. She would not kiss Clinton Marks again. Not in the dark. Not in a park.

The impromptu rhyme made her smile.

And if *he* kissed her instead?

As much as she might wish otherwise, if that ever happened, then all bets were off.

Because she might just have to kiss him back.

CHAPTER TEN

"You used to have an earring in high school."

A swallow of his milk shake went down the wrong way, and Clint gave a couple of rough coughs before turning in his seat to stare at her. In the dim light of the parking lot at a nearby burger joint, he could just make out her questioning gaze. He'd decided against going to the park, worried about being *too* alone with her.

This was more public, although he wasn't exactly sure what he was worried about. Surely they could both handle this situation like adults. Running into each other from time to time was part of adult behavior.

And going to the fair and having dinner with her and her mother?

All part of being back in his hometown. It meant nothing. At least, he'd better make sure it didn't.

And what about her asking about his earring?

Jessi must have changed clothes before leaving the hospital, because she wasn't wearing a lab jacket or rubber-soled shoes but a pair of slim, dark jeans, lime-green T-shirt and a pair of shoes that had a wedged heel. Not what he would consider doctor gear at all. In fact, she looked much more like the teenager he'd known in high school than a mom with a grown daughter.

He felt like an old fuddy-duddy in comparison, still

in his shirt and tie. He could have sworn the kid at the drive-through window had eyed Jessi with interest. Clint had thrown the teen a glare in return, which had felt like something Jessi's actual father might have done.

When had he turned into such a square?

Maybe when he'd seen the emotional wounds of those returning from battle. And how they reminded him of his own.

"I did have an earring. I took it out the night before I reported for boot camp."

The night of their graduation. The night he'd made love to Jessi. It had marked the end of an era for him, a journey from childhood to becoming a man. Removing the earring that night had been something the old Clint wouldn't have done. He'd have reported to boot camp and waited until someone ordered him to take it out. But he hadn't. After watching Jessi's house for a while that night, he'd gone home—avoiding the after parties and festivities that had gone along with graduation—and stared at himself in the bathroom mirror. God, he'd wanted to stay in Richmond that night. For the first time he'd thought of doing something other than running away. And it had been all because of Jessi.

Instead, he'd unhooked the small gold hoop and pulled it from his ear. As if that one act would give him the courage to walk away when everything inside him had been yelling at him to stay and fight for her, shoving aside his fears about what might happen if he did. What kind of life he might drag her into, if he stayed.

But, even if he'd decided to risk it all for her, Jessi was already spoken for, at least according to Larry and all their friends.

The image in the mirror that night had told him which of them had had a better shot of giving Jess a good life. The choice had been obvious—at least to him. He had just been a screwup from a dysfunctional family, his finger a constant reminder of what that brought.

He hadn't wanted that for her.

So he'd let her go. An act his teenage self had decided was the mature thing to do. He still had that old hoop in a box somewhere.

Jessi unexpectedly reached up, her fingers cool from holding her frozen drink as they touched his chin. Using gentle pressure, she turned his head to the right, leaning over to look. Her breath washed across his skin, the scent of vanilla catching hold of his senses and making him want to sneak a taste of her mouth.

"Is there still a hole where your earring used to be?"

What was with all the questions? And why had he ever thought sitting in a car—or anywhere else—with her was a good idea?

Just being an adult. Proving he could control his impulses.

He swallowed. "I haven't really looked in a while. Why?"

"We had a guy come into the ER tonight who'd hooked himself while fishing and I had to push the barb all the way through his ear. He was worried his family would think he'd pierced it." She gave a soft laugh. "He wanted to know how long it would take to heal. I told him he should be more worried about the risk of tetanus than a tiny hole."

Her nose wrinkled. "The worst thing was there was still a live worm attached to the end of that hook."

"Well, that had to be an interesting scenario."

"I almost couldn't do it." She let go of him and leaned back in her seat. "Did you ever have to do something and wonder if you'd be able to get through it?" She made a sound in her throat. "Never mind. Of course you have."

He could think of two at the moment. One was leaving her behind twenty-two years ago. And the other was not touching her now, when everything inside him was straining to do just that. "I think everyone eventually gets a case like that. Or at least wonders if the patient would be better off with another doctor."

Jessi suddenly bent to get her milk shake. In the process the lid came off, dumping the cup, and half of its contents, right onto her lap.

He moved to grab it just as her cry of dismay went up. "Oh, no. Clint, I'm so sorry. Your car."

"I'm more worried about you turning into a block of ice." He sent her a half grin as he tried to scoop some of the shake back into the cup. It only ended up sloshing more onto her shirt and jeans.

"Don't move." He got out of the car, cup in hand, and strode into the restaurant to throw it away, exiting a few seconds later with a fresh empty cup and a handful of napkins.

Together they corralled most of the spillage between the paper cup and a spare lid, and then sopped up the remainder with the pile of napkins.

"I always was the clumsiest girl in high school."

"Don't do that."

"What?"

"You used to cut yourself down for things, even when they weren't your fault."

He could always remember some self-deprecating comment or other she would throw out there in school, making everyone laugh and passing it off as a big joke. But there had always been a ring of conviction to the jibes that had made him wonder if she didn't actually believe all the "I'm such a klutzo" and "Wow, am I ever a nerd" statements.

She glanced up at him, her hand full of napkins. "Everyone did that. Even you."

Yes, he had. And he knew for a fact that he'd believed

most of what he'd said. Maybe that's why it bothered him so much when she did it.

"Let's get you home."

"I'll pay for whatever it costs to clean your seats."

He shook his head. "They're leather. I'll just wipe them down with a damp rag. They'll be fine. You, however, might need to be hosed off." He said it with a grin to show he was joking.

"Thanks for being so understanding," she said, as he gathered up the rest of the trash and got out of the car once more to throw it all away.

Understanding? Hell, he was barely holding it together. He put the car in Drive and followed her directions to her house. "Come on in while I change. We can talk about Chelsea over coffee, if that's okay?"

"Sounds good."

No, it didn't. It sounded idiotic. Impulsive. And he should leave. Now. But something drove him to open his car door and follow her up the steps to her house.

It's just coffee. She hasn't propositioned you. You're her daughter's doctor, for God's sake.

He was the one who'd called to arrange this meeting in the first place.

Which meant he should have asked her to come to his office, not a fast-food joint.

But surely Jessi had patients who were acquaintances or the children of acquaintances during her years of working in the ER. And it would make sense that she might meet them in the hospital cafeteria or a coffee joint to catch up later. It was kind of hard to work in a town where you grew up—no matter how large—and never expect to run into anyone you knew.

Only Jessi was more than an acquaintance.

And what they'd had was more than a quick hello and goodbye.

That was years ago. They'd spent a little over an hour down by a creek, hopped up on hormones and the thrill of graduating from high school. And she'd been distraught by her father's unbending rules.

It was in the past. All of it.

And that kiss beside his car at her mother's house a week ago?

Fueled by memories of that shared past. It wouldn't happen again. Not if he could help it.

She unlocked the door, glancing behind her as if to make sure he was still coming. "I'll get you that rag if you want to wipe the seat down while I change. I'll leave the front door open."

"Sounds good." And if he were smart, he'd leave the rag just outside the door afterwards and take off in his car before she could come back out of her bedroom.

And that would be just as unprofessional as kissing her had been.

At least that was his mental excuse, because after wiping up the few drops of milk shake from his seat he found himself back inside her house, calling up the stairs to her and asking her what she wanted him to do with the rag.

"Just put it in the sink and have a seat in the living room. I'll be down in a few minutes."

Instead of doing as she asked, he rinsed out the rag and hung it over a towel bar he found in her utility room. Then he spotted the coffee machine on one of the counters and a huge glass jar filled with those single-serving coffee filters that seemed to be all the rage nowadays. He had one of the machines at home himself. The least he could do was make the coffee while he waited. He'd just found the mugs when Jessi came traipsing back into the kitchen, this time dressed in a white floral sundress similar to the one she'd worn during dinner at her mom's, her feet bare, hair damp as if she'd showered.

He tensed, before forcing himself to relax again.

Of course she'd had to rinse off. She'd had a sticky drink spilled in her lap. It meant nothing.

"Sorry, Clint. I didn't intend you to get the coffee ready, too."

"No problem. I just thought I'd save you a step." He realized something. "Where's Cooper?"

"At Mom's. He's a communal pet, remember? I get him tomorrow."

"Ah, right."

She reached in a cabinet. "What do you take in your coffee?"

"Just sugar."

She set a crystal bowl down and then went over to the refrigerator and pulled out a container of milk. "Help yourself."

"Thanks."

They worked in silence until the coffee was done and they'd moved into Jessi's living room, which was furnished with a huge sectional and a center ottoman. Pictures lined the fireplace mantel and as he took a sip of his coffee he wandered over to them. There were several snapshots of Chelsea doing various activities and one of a more formal military pose. She was soft and natural in every photo except the last one, since official portraits were supposed to be done sans smile. But even in that one there was a spark of humor lighting her eyes that the woman back at the VA hospital lacked.

There was one picture of Jessi and Larry in their wedding attire. Both of them looked so young. Larry would be forever ageless, never having had a chance to really grow up and become a man.

He might still be alive if someone hadn't...

Her earlier words came back to mind. If he *were* still

alive, Clint would probably not be standing here in her living room right now.

He probably shouldn't be, regardless.

And the sight of the two of them smiling up at each other sent something kicking at his innards. A slight jabbing sensation that could have been jealousy but that made no sense. He'd been the one who'd left. What had he expected Jessi to do? Dump Larry and wait for him to come back for her?

He hadn't. He'd never set foot in Virginia again until now. And if he'd known who Chelsea was before he'd agreed to come, he doubted very seriously he would be standing here now.

"Clint?"

Her voice reminded him that he was still staring at the picture. "Sorry. Just seeing how Chelsea was before she deployed." He turned and sat on the shorter leg of the sofa perpendicular to her. "She smiled a lot."

"Yes. She was happy. Always. Which is why it's so hard to see her like this and not know how to help her."

"I'm sure it is." He took another sip of his coffee, wishing he hadn't added quite so much sugar.

"Did she talk at all today?" Jessi tucked her legs up under her, smoothing her hemline to cover her bare knees.

"She shared a little about what her days in captivity had been like. What she did to pass the time."

"You said on the phone there weren't any breakthroughs. You don't consider that one?"

That was a tricky question to answer. Because while it was technically more than Chelsea had told him in the past, she'd spoken without emotion, as if she were using the information itself as one more blockade against questions that might venture too close to painful subjects. Like that macabre tissue paper baby she kept in her nightstand.

"It does help to know a little about what went on. But

she's not talking about her captors or about her rescue. Just about what she did. Reciting her ABCs and having conversations inside her head."

Jessi slumped. "It's been almost two and a half months."

He didn't mention that sometimes the effects of PTSD lasted a lifetime. His dad, instead of getting better, had slowly sunk into a pit filled with alcohol, drawing away from those he'd known and loved. And when he or his mom had tried to force the issue… Yeah, that was something he didn't want to talk to Jessi about.

"I know it seems like forever. But she was held for four months. It takes time. Sometimes lots of it."

She stared down at her cup for several long seconds before glancing up with eyes that held a wealth of pain. "It sounds so terrible for me to say this out loud, but I'm afraid to have her home again. Afraid the next time she tries something I won't get there in time to stop her."

Clint set his coffee cup down on a tray that was perched on an ottoman between the two seating areas. He went over to sit beside her, setting her coffee aside as he draped his arm around her shoulder and drew her close. "Jess, you're dealing with some aftereffects yourself. Maybe you should talk to someone."

She lifted her head. "I'm talking to you."

"I mean someone objective." The second the words came out of his mouth he wished he could haul them back and swallow them whole. He tried to clarify his meaning. "It would be a conflict of interest for me to treat you both."

He realized that explanation wasn't any better when she tried to pull away from him. He squeezed slightly, keeping her where she was. "I'm not explaining myself very well." Hell, some psychiatrist he was. He couldn't even have a coherent conversation with this woman.

"No, it's okay." She relaxed, and her arm snaked around his waist with a sigh. "I'm being overly sensitive."

No, she wasn't. And Clint was drawing closer and closer to a line he'd sworn he wasn't going to cross with her. But with her head against his chest and her hand curled around his side, her scent surrounded him. *She* surrounded him.

Her fingers went to his left hand and her head lifted slightly, staring at something. Then she touched his damaged finger. She bent a little closer. "What happened?"

Damn. He tried to laugh it off. "An old war wound."

"You never mentioned going to war."

He hadn't. That particular war had been fought here on American soil. Not even his father had known what he'd done to his son with that hard, angry squeeze.

"I was making a joke. A bad one." He shrugged. "It's not important."

Her head went back to his chest, but her finger continued to stroke his crooked pinkie, the sensation strangely intimate and disturbing on a level that was primal.

He needed to get up and move before either of them did something they would regret.

Then she lifted his hand to her mouth and kissed his finger, the delicate touch ramming through his chest and driving the air from his lungs.

Her tongue trailed across the skin, and his hand tightened slightly on her shoulder. He wasn't sure whether or not it was in warning. And if it was, was he warning her not to stop? Or not to continue? His body responded to the former, rejecting the latter. Because he did want her to continue. To keep on kissing him with those featherlight brushes. And not just there. Everywhere.

"Jess," he murmured. "I think I should move back to the other seat."

She stopped, still holding his hand. "Does that mean you're going to?" Her whispered words were as much a caress as her touch had been.

Heat swirled through him.

"Not if you keep talking to me in that tone of voice."

She let go of his hand and moved hers a little bit higher, smoothing over his biceps until her palm rested on his shoulder. And when she looked up at him, he was lost.

Decision made.

He was going to kiss her. Just like she'd kissed him. Softly. Gently. And with just enough contact to drive her wild.

CHAPTER ELEVEN

IT WAS AS if the past twenty-two years had rewound themselves.

The second his lips touched hers, Jessi was back by the creek, her only worries her father's strict rules and getting to school on time. And it felt so good. So carefree.

If only she'd known how free she'd been back then.

But she could experience it again. With the same man. Just for a little while.

She'd always thought Clint had been invincible all those years ago. But her mom's comment about his father and discovering that crooked little finger showed her he wasn't. He was just as human as she was. Back then…and maybe even now.

Jessi threaded her fingers through his hair, hearing Clint's low groan as he moved to deepen the kiss, shifting her until she lay half across his lap, one of his hands beneath her shoulders, his other splayed flat on her stomach. It was that hand that made her go all liquid inside. It wasn't doing anything special but it was between two very sensitive areas of her body, both of which were doing their damnedest to coax his fingers to slide their way.

A gentle touch of his tongue was enough to get her full attention.

Yes!

Surely he wouldn't stop this time. It had been ages since she'd been with someone. So long that the slightest movement of his body had her eagerly lapping up the sensations like a person deprived of food and water, and desperate for any sign of relief.

She was ready for that kind of relief. For him.

Clint.

And here he was, in her house. And there was absolutely no one around. Not her mom. Not Chelsea.

Just the two of them.

So she pressed closer to him, deepening their kiss, his soft lips making her feel dizzy with need.

And finally…finally, the hand at her waist woke up, his thumb drawing little circles on her belly that had her moaning with anticipation, arching up into it with a mental plea that he evidently heard. Because with a single movement it slid up and over her right breast, that circling thumb finding her nipple without hesitation. Her sundress had a built-in bra, but it was thin, just a shelf of netting with a piece of elastic beneath it, so his touch was heady and intimate, arcing straight down to her toes and then back up again.

When his fingers moved away, she whimpered in protest. His mouth slid from hers, depriving her of another point of contact.

"Clint…"

His hand moved to the back of her head, supporting it as the scrape of his chin along her cheek put him at her ear. "I don't want to stop."

The moment of truth. She sensed he was giving her time to compose herself, to give her a chance to put an end to things even while telling her he didn't want to.

She made a dangerous decision.

"Then don't."

His fingers tightened on the back of her head. Then

his other hand went to the thin strap on her sundress and tugged it down her arm, leaving one shoulder bare.

There was a slight hesitation, then that wicked thumb went to work, brushing the joint where her shoulder met her arm. "Is this what you want?"

"More." The word came out as a shaky whisper. She hardly dared to believe she was goading him to continue. But this was exactly what she needed. To have someone just sweep aside her normal code of conduct and make her...*feel* again.

"How about this?" His fingertips moved higher, trailing from beneath her jaw down the side of her neck and along her collarbone. Light ticklish touches that made her ache and squirm.

She wanted him everywhere at once, kissing her mouth, cupping her breast, filling her with his heat where it counted the most. So she took his hand and placed it on her breast, where she wanted it.

"You read my mind, Jess." The words came out in a half growl that made her shiver.

He ducked beneath the edge of her sundress and found her bare skin. He paused then curved his palm over her, the light friction on her nipple sending a low sound up her throat.

"Hell, woman. You need to warn a man before you go braless."

Encouraged by the rough words, she bit her way up his jaw and then smiled against his mouth. "My dress has a bra. You just missed it."

"Could have fooled me." His thumb and forefinger captured the tight bead and gave a gentle squeeze that made her squirm again. "But in that case..."

He removed his hand and urged her off the couch and onto her feet, while he sat, legs splayed.

"Wh-what are you doing?"

"I want to see you—all of you—but at the rate I'm going, I'm not going to make it that far." A quick flash of teeth accompanied the words.

She smiled back at him, his meaning giving her a shot of courage and daring her to tease him back. "I think I can help with that. What would you like to see first?" Balling the skirt portion of her dress, she slid the hem part way up her thighs, keeping her attention focused on his face.

A muscle worked in his jaw, and he placed his hands flat on his thighs. "Let's start from the top. And work our way down. Just like we did in school."

The reminder of how his hands had trailed from her face to her breasts and finally down to that last forbidden place made hot need spurt through her. And the way his knuckles turned white as his long fingers dug into his thighs told her that need wasn't one-sided.

"Okay, let's do that." She let go of her skirt and trailed the back of her right hand down her neck, like he'd done moments earlier, only she didn't stop at her collarbone. Instead, she dragged her fingers along the edge of her bodice—one strap still draped over her arm. The second strap flipped down.

"Next?" she asked, waiting for direction.

"Peel it down. Slowly." The low words weren't abrupt and bossy, rather they coaxed her to do his bidding. Dared her to cross a threshold to a room she'd never entered before. Her times with Larry had been good, but they'd been to the point. Vanilla sex that had been a sharing of hearts and minds, even if it hadn't been superimaginative. Then again, they'd had such a short amount of time together, there hadn't been a chance to venture much further than that.

And that wasn't something she was going to think about.

Not when Clint was right here, holding the door open and asking her to step through it.

This was what she wanted—what she expected from Clint. Wild and raw and real...echoes of the rebellious boy he'd once been. The one who had whispered to a matching defiance within her, drawing it out and fulfilling her in ways she never would have imagined.

So she crossed her arms and took a strap in each hand and pulled with slow, steady pressure that made the fabric of her dress roll back on itself, revealing the upper swell of her breasts. She kept going until she got to the most crucial part, then hesitated.

"Jess." The whispered word shifted her eyes back to his. But he wasn't looking at her face. He was staring at the half-exposed portion of her body, the heat in his expression taking away the last of her inhibitions. She tugged, and he swallowed.

"You have no idea how much I want to drag you down here and finish this."

"Then do it." She let her arms go to her sides, making no attempt to hide herself from him.

He reached behind him and retrieved his wallet from his pants. Her mouth watered, thinking he was going to pull a condom out and do exactly what she'd suggested. And a packet did appear, but he made no move to haul her down onto the couch.

"Here or in your bedroom?"

"It doesn't matter." It was the truth. She wanted him. Badly, and she didn't care where it happened, as long as it happened. And soon.

He smiled again and set the condom on his thigh, making her tighten inside. Because six inches north of that packet was a bulge that left no question as to whether or not he wanted her.

"Does that dress have a zipper?"

It took a second for the question to register, and when she glanced up at him she saw that he knew exactly where she'd been looking. That he'd meant for her to measure the distance between possibility and reality. Because nothing was for sure until he slipped that protection over himself and thrust into her.

"Yes."

"Can you reach it?"

She nodded, her now shaking fingers going to the side of her dress, finding the pull tab then sliding it down to her hips, her other hand holding the rest of the garment in place.

"Let it go," he murmured, his meaning clear.

Releasing her grip, the fabric slid to the floor, leaving her standing in front of him clad only in her panties.

She expected him to tell her to remove those as well, but instead his fingers went to the button of his slacks and undid it.

"Once those come off, honey, it's all over." His bald words made the breath stall in her chest. As did the fact that he was sliding his own zipper down and ripping the condom open.

She wanted to do that. "Wait."

Wary eyes moved to her face. Oh! He thought she was stopping him.

Hurrying to correct him, she said, "Let me."

He took the condom from the packet. "Next time."

Next time!

Her lips parted as he drew the waistband to his briefs down and exposed himself. And unlike her, Clint had no inhibitions. None. Not the last time they'd been together. Not this time. His eyes burned into hers as he sat there. He toyed with the open condom.

The nub at the apex of her thighs tightened, making her squeeze her legs together, aching for some kind of relief.

She licked her lips. "Put it on."

"First your panties."

Hurrying to do as he asked, she hooked her thumbs into the elastic and started to bend over to slide them down, only to have him interrupt her. "Watch me as you do it."

Shifting her focus back to his face, she finished, stepping out of her underwear and standing back upright.

"Beautiful," he murmured. "Even more now than then."

He finally rolled the condom down his length, and took himself in hand. "Now come here, honey."

She moved between his still splayed legs and shuddered when the fingers of his free hand slid in a smooth move up her thigh and found the heart of her. Just the process of removing her clothing while he'd watched had made her body moist and ready.

"Hell. Just like I remember."

By the time he'd finally touched her by the creek, she'd been shaking with desire. One flick of his finger had sent her over the edge. She'd been so embarrassed, only to have him shush her and tell her how much he liked it. When he'd finally entered her, she had already been riding the crest of that same wave, shattering right along with him.

The Clint of today slid one finger inside her, wringing a moan from her. He stayed there, just like that, not moving. She shuddered, needing him so badly she couldn't speak.

"Spread your legs for me."

Somehow, she shuffled her legs farther apart.

"Perfect." He sat up straight, the pressure of his finger inside her holding her right where she was, putting his face dangerously close. Too late, she realized that was what he'd been aiming for all along. "How much will it take this time, Jess?"

Another reference to their first time together.

He added a second finger and pushed deep, using the pair to edge her hips closer. Suddenly off balance, she was forced to clutch his shoulders. "How much, Jess?" he repeated.

Then, as she watched, he moved his mouth until it was pressed against her…and let his tongue slide right across her.

It was as if he'd lit a fuse inside her. Her nails dug into his shoulders and every muscle in her body stiffened as what he was doing blotted out everything except the sensation of his tongue moving backward along her in a slow, drawn-out motion. The fuse ran out of line in a millisecond, and she detonated, crying out as his fingers finally moved, pumping inside her while she convulsed around them.

Then she was in his lap, his hands gripping her butt as he thrust hard into her, filling her beyond belief. She wrapped her hands around his neck, her mouth going to his ear as she rode him furiously, whimpering as her climax continued to crash all around her. He gave a muttered oath and then jerked his hips forward, holding her tight against his body as he strained upward for long seconds, the pressure inside her causing a new wave of convulsions.

When his muscles finally went limp, his arms encircled her back, thumb gliding along her spine.

She drew a deep, careful breath, registered Clint's heavy breathing and smiled, the problems of the day melting as his scent mixed with her own and filled her head. She nuzzled his cheek and then went back to his ear.

"I guess I'm not the only one who went up pretty fast."

His fingers tightened around her, although his voice was light. "Is that a complaint?"

"No. It was sexy, watching you lose control."

He drew her mouth back to his and kissed her long and deep. "Is that so? In that case, maybe we should find out which one of us holds out longer…the second time around."

CHAPTER TWELVE

"It's just been a long time, and I was upset."

Not the first words a man wanted to hear when he woke up after a night of passionate lovemaking. But there they were, and Clint was at an obvious disadvantage, since he was lying on her couch, an afghan draped over his privates, while Jessi hovered above him, already dressed, looking both worried and...

Hungry.

It was there in her eyes as they slid over his body and then darted back to his face, as if she was doing her damnedest not to look at him.

They'd never even made it back to her bedroom last night, instead using the long L-shaped couch to its full advantage.

Well, if she thought he was going to make it easy for her...

He slid up and propped himself up one of the throw pillows as he eyed her right back.

"Well, that's a hell of a good morning."

She took a step closer. "Sorry. I just don't want you to think..."

"That last night meant something other than great sex?"

Her eyes widened. "That's not what I was going to say."

"So it did mean something," he said, not sure which he preferred.

"No." She held out a hand to stop him from saying anything else. All that did, though, was give him a way to reach out grab her wrist.

She half laughed, half screamed. "Clint, stop. I'm trying to be serious."

"Oh, honey, so am I."

She let him drag her to the sofa and haul her down on top of him, where a certain area of his body was already displaying its delight at this turn of events.

"Wait. Let me finish my thought."

Leaving his fingers threaded in her hair, he looked at her, knowing his next words were not what he wanted to say at all. Hell, he didn't want her to say *anything* except what she wanted him to do to her. But he forced the words out. "Okay, so talk."

She drew an audible breath. "I just didn't want you to think last night had anything to do with Chelsea."

Her eyes trailed away from him, but the words themselves hit him in the chest like a bucket of ice water, sluicing away any hint of desire and leaving a cold trail of suspicion in its wake.

A sour taste rose up in his throat.

"I hadn't thought that at all, Jess." He rolled until she was wedged between him and the back of the couch as he stared at her. "Until just this very second. Did last night have something to do with her?"

"No! Yes. There are just things that you don't know. About how her father...about how Larry died. Not even Chelsea knows. But if someone from our past sees you, I'm afraid she could find out."

"I think you'd better tell me, then."

Jessi's eyes filled with tears. "A few months after we got married he told one of his friends I was pregnant. Well, the friend had seen us—you and me—leave graduation together and come back within minutes of each other. It got him thinking. He suggested Larry ask me whose child I was carrying." There was a pause before she continued. "We had a huge fight, and he accused me of sleeping with you. When I wouldn't deny it, he said Chelsea probably wasn't even his."

She shifted against the couch, and he eased back to give her some breathing space.

Clint could barely open his mouth. "His death?"

"He stormed off...so very angry. He went to a bar, and then a few hours later his car hit an embankment. He died instantly."

Hell. He felt like the biggest ass in history.

He leaned his forehead against hers, guilt causing his muscles to cramp. One more thing destroyed by his lack of control all those years ago. "Dammit. I'm sorry, Jessi. I had no idea."

So many mistakes: if he hadn't impulsively raced after her that night. If he hadn't stayed there with her and done the unthinkable... If he hadn't left her to deal with it all afterwards.

The small box of baggage from the past morphed into a shiny new trunk of regret.

They remained like that for a minute or two until Jessi gave a little sniff.

He scooted back some more, giving her a chance to compose herself, trying to ignore the quick swipe of palms across damp cheeks. The last thing he wanted to do was hurt her.

Then...or now. But it would seem he'd done both.

And he knew what he had to do to keep from hurting her further.

He sat up and slid off the sofa, conscious of her eyes following his movements as he gathered his clothing and headed for the bathroom just down her hallway. After he'd flushed and washed his hands, he dressed quickly, avoiding his image in the mirror as much as he possibly could, because whenever his eyes met those in the reflection, angry accusations stared right back at him.

How had he let this happen again?

When he was around her, his common sense went out the window, and he let his emotions rule.

Just like his father. He didn't hit, but his actions caused just as much damage. Dammit, they'd culminated in a young man's death. Someone Jessi had loved.

He had to take himself off Chelsea's case. It was no longer about remaining objective but about doing what had served him—and everyone around him—well for the last twenty-two years: staying away from emotionally charged situations.

If he'd known the details about Larry's death, he would have taken himself off Chelsea's case that very first day. This time, though, he wasn't going to let Jessi carry any of the blame for what just had happened between them. Nope, he was going to stuff it into his own bag of blame. One that seemed to swell larger every time he laid eyes on her. When he returned to the living room, Jessi was still there, seated on the sofa, only this time she had a phone to her ear.

"Of course, honey," Jessi said to whoever was on the line. "I'll check with Dr. Marks and see how soon we can arrange it." Her glance met his and she mouthed, "Chelsea."

Jessi's daughter was calling her? Right now?

He sat beside her, suddenly very aware of all inappropriate things they'd done in this house last night.

The second she clicked off the phone, she finally looked at him. Really looked at him. "Chelsea wants to talk about something." She licked her lips as if afraid of saying the next words. "She wants us both to be there."

* * *

Please, don't quit yet.

The words chanted through her skull as Clint dropped her off at Scott's Memorial to pick up her car and then waited for her to follow him back to the VA hospital.

They hadn't said much once she'd got off the phone, and the interior of his car had been filled with awkward silence and a sense of dread that had blocked her stomach and clogged her throat.

How could she have been so stupid to think last night wouldn't have any serious repercussions? Her only excuse was that it had felt so good to be in his arms. So right.

Only it wasn't right.

The timing had always been lousy when it came to her and Clint. If he'd stayed all those years ago, she never would have married Larry. But she never would have had Chelsea either.

And just like last time Clint wouldn't be there for the long haul. As soon as they'd found a replacement for him, he'd be gone.

He would waltz out of her life once again.

It's just not meant to be. It never was.

The words trailed through her head as if dragged on a banner behind a plane for all the world to see.

Her subconscious rejected them, though, cutting the line and watching as the lettering fell to the ground in a swirl of white canvas and belching smoke.

Before she had a chance to come to any conclusions, Clint pulled to a stop in one of the few parking spaces that had another spot beside it. She slid her car next to his and took a couple of deep breaths before she got out and went to where he stood, waiting. "You won't say anything, will you?"

Clint looked at her as if she had two heads. "About

what? Larry? Or about us having a second one-night stand?"

A flash of intense hurt zinged through her chest, making her gasp for air.

As if realizing what he'd done, he hooked his index finger around hers. "Sorry, Jess." He gave a squeeze before letting her go. "I seem to spend a lot of time issuing apologies nowadays."

She tipped her chin back. "Let's just see what she wants." The words came out sharper than she'd meant them to, but maybe that was a good thing. She could put her armor back in place and pretend last night had meant nothing. "We can discuss everything else later. If we could avoid arriving at her room at the same time, that would make me feel more comfortable."

"So you want me to hide out in my office for a few minutes before joining you."

Saying it like that made Jessi realize how cheesy and paranoid the idea sounded. "You're right. Let's just go together."

Once they got to Chelsea's room, they found her seated on the bed, that eerie tissue-paper baby on top of the nightstand. Jessi tensed. That had to be what she wanted to talk about.

She leaned down and kissed her cheek. "Hi, sweetheart."

Chelsea grabbed her around the shoulders, wordlessly hugging her tight for a minute or two. Then she whispered, "I'm sorry for putting you through what I have for the past couple of months. I love you, Mom. Always remember that."

A chill went over her at the solemn words. She stood up and glanced at Clint. "All that matters is that you start feeling better."

"I think I will as soon as I get something off my chest."

Once they were all seated, Clint started things off with some light conversation, never even hinting that he'd been with Jessi in anything other than a professional capacity. Instead, he asked about Jessi's day at work yesterday, subtly guiding her to tell the fishhook-in-the-ear story. Chelsea actually laughed right on cue.

"You hate worms," her daughter said.

"I do. I still remember you bringing in a jar of dirt for me on Mother's Day. Little did I know that that you and Grandpa had spent hours digging up earthworms to put in it."

Chelsea grinned again. "You screamed when one of them dug through the dirt and slithered along the inside of the jar. Grandpa laughed and laughed."

Jessi smiled at the memory of Chelsea and her dad's conspiratorial glances at each other as they'd handed her their "gift."

"You always were the fearless one."

"Not always." Chelsea's smile faded. "I need to tell you something. Something about when I was held in Afghanistan."

"Okay." She glanced at Clint, but he simply nodded at her.

Setting the doll in her lap, Chelsea took a deep breath. "You were right about my pregnancy. I was expecting when I was captured. I hadn't told anyone because it meant a ticket straight home—and I didn't want that. The whole thing was so stupid. It was an accident. I kept meaning to do something—say something—but I put things off... and put things off." Her eyes came up. "And then we were ambushed."

Jessi's heart contracted. "Did they...did they do something to you, honey?"

"No." Chelsea glanced up at the ceiling her eyes filling with tears and spilling over. "I mean, they didn't hurt me physically. They isolated me and made me change into a long, loose tunic. Then they wrote a script and forced me to read it in front of a camera."

Jessi had never heard about any message, but she didn't say anything, just let Chelsea continue talking.

"As one month turned into two, the isolation started to get to me, and I began talking to the baby. Every day. I went from just wanting her to go away to needing her for my own survival."

Her?

Oh, God, had they made Chelsea deliver the baby and then stolen it from her? Was that what the doll was all about?

When Chelsea's words stopped, Clint voiced the question that Jessi couldn't bring herself to ask.

"What happened to the baby?" The line of his jaw was tight, as if he too was struggling with his emotions right now.

"She died."

"Oh, Chelsea..." Her mind went blank as she tried to find the words to say. But there was nothing.

"She died, and I couldn't do anything to save her."

"Your captors didn't help?"

She shook her head. "I didn't want them to know I was pregnant, because I wasn't sure how they'd react to an unmarried woman carrying a child. So I hid my condition. It wasn't hard under the robes. I was in my cell most of the time, and I figured once I delivered, they'd let me keep her, or maybe even let us go."

Clint spoke up. "How far along were you when you were captured?"

"Around three months." She turned to glance at him. "I lost track of time after a while, but I think she was born around four months into my captivity."

Too small. Without the help of modern medicine the baby wouldn't have had much chance to survive.

Chelsea continued. "She came in the middle of the night. She was so tiny. And absolutely perfect." Her fingers caressed the doll. "She never even cried. I held her for a long, long time, praying for her to take a breath." Her voice broke for a second, but then she continued. "After a while, I knew she was dead, and I was afraid if anyone found out, I'd be killed, too—and I didn't want anyone other than me touching her. So I tore off a piece of my robe and wrapped her in it, then I scratched a hole in the dirt floor of my cell with my fingernails and buried her. I was rescued less than a week later."

A couple more tears trickled free, and Jessi reached over and held her hand, her own vision blurry.

"I'm so, so sorry, Chelsea." Her daughter had dealt with all of this by herself. There'd been no one there to help her...no one to comfort her. Her own heart felt ready to shatter in two.

A box of tissues appeared on the tiny table in front of them. Chelsea took several of them and wiped her eyes and then blew her nose before turning to look at her.

"Once she was gone, I realized just how alone I was. I couldn't even mark my baby's grave. And if I died there, I would be just like her. Dumped in a shallow grave somewhere. No one would even know I existed. After I got home, I started thinking maybe that would be for the best. That the baby should have survived. Not me. That I should be the one forgotten, instead of her."

Clint leaned forward. "You wouldn't have been forgotten, Chelsea. People would have grieved deeply, just like you grieved for your baby. You have a mother who loves you. A grandmother. Comrades in your unit. And you're right where you should be. You're here. Alive. Everything you did while in that cell had to be done. It gave you a chance to survive. Gave you a chance to make sure your baby would never be forgotten.

"If you had died, her memory would have died with you." He paused, keeping his gaze focused on her. "And yet look at what's happened. Your mom now knows about her. I know about her. You'll probably talk to more people about her as you live your life. She won't be forgotten. Your very survival makes that a certainty."

Chelsea seemed to consider his words for a minute, and then nodded as if coming to a decision. "I'd like her to have a grave here in the States. A marker with her name on it."

"Of course we'll do that." Jessi wondered if the ache in her heart would ever stop. She'd been about to be a grandmother of a baby girl who might have survived, given access to modern medical facilities. But those were things she could never say to Chelsea—*would* never say to her. They would decide together whether to tell Chelsea's paternal grandparents. Larry's parents were still alive, and Jessi and Chelsea kept in touch with them regularly. As for her mother...

They could think through all that later. The important thing was that Chelsea was talking. Working through things she hadn't told another soul.

She had to ask. "Does the father know?"

"No. I never told him, and there seems to be no point now." She licked her lips. "And he could get in serious trouble if the truth were made known."

"Why?"

"He's an officer, and I'm not. We weren't supposed to get involved with each other to begin with."

Jessi shot Clint a glance that was probably just as guilt-filled as she feared. But he wasn't looking at her. At all.

"Did you love him?"

"No. And he didn't love me. It just happened. Neither of

us meant for it to, and we've never gotten together again. It was just the one time."

God. Chelsea could have been describing exactly what had happened years ago, only with different players. And Chelsea was right about one thing. Larry had found out and the consequences had been disastrous. And so very permanent.

Her stomach clenched and clenched.

And unlike Chelsea, she hadn't learned from that mistake all those years ago. She'd gone right back and done it again.

Jessi hadn't been able to resist Clint.

She never had. He'd been just as taboo as that officer Chelsea had spoken of.

Chelsea glanced at Clint. "You told me during our first meeting that you were here to help me get through this. So I'm ready to try. I promise to work really hard."

Clint stiffened visibly in his seat.

Chelsea, totally unaware of the strained dynamics in the room, kept on talking. "Did you go through boot camp, Dr. Marks?"

"I did." Nothing in his voice betrayed his feelings, but Jessi knew. She knew exactly the struggle going on inside him right now.

"Then you know a soldier agrees never to leave a wounded comrade behind."

He gave a quick nod.

"I may not be missing a limb or have any visible external injuries except these…" she held out her wrists, showing the scars "…but I am wounded. So please, please don't leave me behind."

CHAPTER THIRTEEN

THEY WERE MAKING PROGRESS.

It came in fits and starts, but the past week had seen Chelsea come further than she had since she'd been at the hospital.

And Clint was still on her case, even though in his heart of hearts he knew he shouldn't be. But Chelsea's words had reached to the heart of who he was as a soldier, and he knew that he would have wished more than anything that someone had been there for his father. But they hadn't. He'd dealt with his demons alone. That's not what he wanted for Chelsea.

Besides, since that session, Jessi had been careful to keep her distance, speaking to him only when he asked her something during joint sessions or when he saw her in the halls at the VA hospital. It was like she was walking on eggshells around him.

Well, so was he, around her. And the edges of those shells were beginning to feel damn uncomfortable beneath his feet.

But as long as he could maintain things for another few weeks, they should be fine. Chelsea had gotten her wish not to be abandoned "like her baby." And she was gradually starting to believe that none of what had happened had been her fault. She'd soon be discharged and start doing her sessions on a weekly outpatient basis—which meant he'd be seeing even less of Jessi.

And that made his chest tighten in ways he'd never thought possible. In fact, he hadn't felt this way since...

Since the day he'd left her twenty-two years ago.

Just like he'd leave her again once his transfer papers went through.

And, yes, he was prepared to put in for one, even though a little voice inside of him whispered that when this was all over—when Chelsea was no longer his patient—he could ask Jessi out on a real date and woo her the way he'd once dreamed about.

Except nothing had changed. Not really.

He was still not the right man for her. He was still too cautious—too afraid to let himself be with any one woman.

Besides, Jessi had already experienced the worst parts of coming from a military family, having a daughter who'd served and come back with serious issues. Did she really need to be involved with a man who dealt with wounded soldiers day after day? Wouldn't it just remind her of all she'd gone through with Chelsea?

Never had he felt the weight of responsibility more than he did right now.

"Dr. Marks?" One of the nurses popped her head into the room. "Peter Summers just called. He's asking for a refill of his methadone prescription."

Another complicated case.

He sighed. Peter's maintenance dosage of the drug was dependent on his showing up for his sessions, the last two of which he'd missed. A longtime addict, methadone was meant to replace cravings. The treatment regimen was highly regulated and required sticking to a precise schedule. That meant outpatient sessions and progress reports. Clint would have followed those guidelines even without the corresponding laws, just because it was the right thing to do.

Hell, it didn't seem like he'd been too worried about doing the right thing when he'd been rolling around on Jessi's couch.

And thoughts like that would get him nowhere.

"Would you mind calling him and setting up a new appointment? Tell him he can't have a refill without coming in."

Consequences. Larry's tragic death came to mind. The consequences of his fling with Jessi.

Well, someone else besides him might as well learn the meaning of the word.

"Will do." The nurse jotted something down onto the paper in her hand. "Oh, and I didn't know if you knew, but there's someone waiting to see you. At least, I think she is. She's come down the hallway and almost knocked on your door twice before going back to the waiting room and just sitting there."

He glanced at his planner. He wasn't scheduled to see anyone for another couple of hours. "Any idea who it is?"

"It's Chelsea Riley's mother."

His throat tightened. Jessi was here to see him? Had almost knocked on his door twice?

"Is she still here?"

The nurse nodded. "She's in the main waiting area."

He pushed his chair back and climbed to his feet. "Has she been to see Chelsea yet?"

"No, that was the strange thing. She came straight here without asking anyone anything." She shrugged. "I thought you might like to know."

"Thank you." He shoved his arms into his sports jacket. "If I'm not in my office when you get hold of Peter Summers, could you leave me note with his next session date? Or let me know what he said?"

"Sure thing."

With that, the nurse popped back out of the room, leaving him to struggle with whether to go down to the waiting area and talk to Jessi or to pretend he knew nothing about it and either wait for her to come to him or to leave, whichever she decided.

Consequences, Clint. You have to do more than talk the talk—you have to be willing to walk the walk. Even if it means walking away.

Despite his inner lecture, he wandered down the hallway—like the idiot he was—and found her in the waiting area, just like Maria had said.

Jessi's head was down, her hands clasped loosely between her jeans-clad knees. She could have been praying. Hell, maybe that's what he should be doing right now. Because just seeing her was like a fist to the stomach. A hard one. Hard enough to leave him breathless and off balance.

And all those emotions he'd worked so hard to suppress boiled up to the surface.

The waiting room was full, only five or six seats empty in the whole place and neither of them next to where Jessi was perched. He moved in, catching the eye of an older man, who, although gaunt, still sat at stiff attention. Clint nodded to him, receiving the same in return. He finally got to where Jessi was seated.

"Jess?"

She glanced up, the worry in her green eyes immediately apparent. She popped to her feet. "I was just coming to see you."

"I know. One of the nurses told me."

Her teeth came down on her lower lip. "I figured it must look weird. I just couldn't get up the nerve to…" She glanced around, bringing back the fact that the room was full and now more than one or two sets of eyes were following their exchange with interest.

"I'll take you back to the office," he said. "And I'll run down to the cafeteria and get us some coffee." He wasn't sure how smart it was to be alone with her. But as long as he kept the door unlocked, they'd be fine. At least, Clint hoped so.

He went to the cafeteria and ordered their coffees. She liked hers with milk, something he shouldn't remember, but did. He dumped a packet of sugar into his own brew and headed back to his office.

When he pushed through the door, he noted she still wore the same haunted expression she'd had earlier. Setting her coffee on the desk in front of her, he went around to the other side and slid into his office chair. "What's going on, Jess?"

"It's Mom. I—I felt like I had to tell her about…about Chelsea's baby, since she and my mom are close." She blinked, maybe seeing something in his face that made her explain further. "I'd already talked to Chelsea about it. She knew I was going to tell her."

"And how did your mom react?"

Her clenched fingers pressed against her chin. "That's just it. She's in the hospital. And I don't know what to tell Chelsea. I know she's going to ask as soon as I go in there."

Shock spurted through his system. "What happened?"

"I think I told you, she hasn't been quite herself lately. Anyway, when she heard the story, she seemed to be handling it okay, then she suddenly started feeling a weird pressure in her chest." Jessi blew out a breath. "It turns out one of her arteries is 90 percent blocked. She needs bypass surgery. She'd been having symptoms for about a month, but didn't want to worry me."

He immediately went to reach for her hand then stopped when Jessi slid hers off the top of the desk and into her lap.

Keeping her distance. Asking for his professional opinion.

Of course that's what it was. She'd already told him what she needed to. She wanted to know whether or not she should tell her daughter about what had happened. She hadn't come to him for comfort or anything else.

Just medical advice about her daughter...his patient.

Right now, though, the last thing he wanted to do was think this thing through. What he wanted was to get out of his chair, walk around the desk and grab her to his chest, holding her while she poured out her heart.

Impulse control.

With his recent track record, holding her was exactly what he shouldn't do.

He took a sip of his coffee and let the heat wash down his throat and pool in his stomach, adding to the acid already there. "I think you should tell her the truth about your mom's condition. Maybe not the events preceding the attack but that her doctor found a blockage in an artery and has decided it needs to be addressed as quickly as possible."

"So you don't think I should tell her about Mom knowing what happened with the baby?"

"Not unless she asks you point-blank. The truth might eventually come out, but I don't think you need to hurry into any kind of explanation right now. That can wait until after the surgery. When your mom—and Chelsea—are better."

The truth might eventually come out.

Great advice, Marks, considering your and Jessi's current situation. And what had happened to her late husband once that truth had indeed come out.

None of that mattered at the moment. "When is the procedure scheduled?"

"They want to do it as soon as possible. This afternoon, in fact."

He sat back in his seat. "Maybe it's good that this happened when it did. At least you were with your mom at the time and knew what to do."

"Did I, Clint? What was I thinking, just blurting something like that out?"

"You said she'd been having symptoms for a while. Besides, I'm sure you didn't 'blurt it out.' You were doing what you thought was best for your mom and for Chelsea."

Like he was doing, by continuing to treat Jessi's daughter? Actually, yes. Nothing had happened to suggest that this couldn't all work out for the best as far as Chelsea was concerned.

"I just never dreamed it might lead to—"

"I know." He paused. "Do you want me to be there when they do the procedure?"

"Don't you have patients?"

Not a direct refusal. More like a hesitation...trying to feel him out, maybe?

"I have one more to see in about an hour and a half. What time is her surgery scheduled for?"

"Five." Her hands came back onto the table and wrapped around her mug.

"I'll be done in plenty of time to get to the hospital." He waited until her eyes came up and met his. "Unless you don't want me there."

There, if she wanted reassurance, he would give it to her. And he had a feeling she could use a friend right now, even if they could never be anything more than that.

"I'd actually like you to be there, if it's not too much trouble."

"Of course it's not."

This time her fingers crept across the desk and touched the top of his hand. He turned his over so it was palm up and curled his fingers around hers.

"Thank you so much, Clint. I know it's hard after everything that went on between us."

"Not hard at all."

They sat there in silence for a few long seconds, hands still gripping each other's. Only now he'd laced his fingers through hers, his thumb stroking over her skin.

A few minutes later she left—with his promise to be at the hospital before her mom's procedure.

And somehow in that period of time he was going to give himself a stern pep talk about what he should and shouldn't do as he sat with her in the waiting room.

And all he could do was hope that—for once—his heart decided to cooperate.

CHAPTER FOURTEEN

JESSI PACED THE waiting room of the hospital an hour into her mom's surgery, her chaotic thoughts charging from one subject to another. Her daughter had been so upset by the news that she hadn't asked if Jessi had told her about the baby.

Or asked any deeper questions about why Jessi had told Clint before she'd told her.

That was good, because the last thing she needed to do was heap one more tricky situation onto the pile.

And tricky was the best way she could think of to characterize her and Clint's relationship.

There was no way she could be falling for Clint all over again. They hadn't seen each other in over twenty years. But as they'd worked together, treating patients at the fair, there'd been a feeling of rightness. A rightness that had continued when they'd made love at her house a week later.

Except feelings didn't always mean anything, at least where she was concerned, because she'd always had a thing for Clint. Even back in high school.

It didn't make a difference then, Jessi, and it's not going to make a difference now. He's going to leave. Just you wait and see.

All those confused feelings had to do with Clint being her first. After all, you never really forgot your first love, right? And she *had* loved Chelsea's father. Very much. If it hadn't been for their argument, Larry would still be alive. Would she even be giving Clint a second glance if he were?

Something else she didn't want to think about because it just made her feel that much worse.

The man in question was seated in one of the cushioned chairs in the hospital waiting room, elbows on his knees, watching her pace. She went over to him. "How do you think it's going?"

One corner of his mouth turned up. "You mean since the last time you asked me? All of five minutes ago?" He patted the chair next to him. "Why don't you sit down? Wearing a hole in the linoleum isn't going to help anyone right now."

She blew out a breath, worry squeezing into every available brain cell and wiping away any other thoughts. Plopping down in the chair, she leaned back and closed her eyes. "What if Mom or Chelsea finds out what we've done?"

"Where did that come from?" His arm went around her shoulders and eased her closer.

"I just don't want to make anything worse for either of them."

"No one's going to find out."

"Larry did." She was immediately sorry she'd said it when his body stiffened.

"Sorry, Clint. I'm just worried."

"I know." He sighed. "You need to stop pacing."

Her eyes opened, and she cranked her head to the right to look at him. "I already did."

"Not there." He nodded at the floor, then his fingers went to her temple and rubbed in slow circles. "I mean up here. You're driving yourself crazy. Nobody's going to find out, unless one of us tells them. And I don't see that happening."

"Thank you," she murmured. "You've been a lot cooler about all of this than I have any right to expect."

He chuckled. "Cool, huh? I don't know if I would call it that, exactly."

She wasn't sure what he meant by that, and she was too nervous to try to figure it out right now. All she knew was that she was glad he was there with her.

Jessi leaned into Clint a little bit more, allowing herself to absorb a little of the confident energy he exuded. That energy was something that had drawn her to him as a high school student, and it wasn't any less potent now.

"How long are they going to be?"

"Jess, it takes time. The doctors felt pretty sure going in that everything was going to run according to plan."

"Yes, but anything could happen." Even as she said it, she allowed her eyelids to slide together, letting his clean scent wash through her, canceling out the sharp bite of disinfectant and illness that came with being at a hospital. She was used to those smells, for the most part, but right now, when she was worried about her mother, they were reminders that sometimes things went wrong, and people died.

"It could, but it probably won't. I think she's going to be just fine."

His words were so inviting, offering up a reality that was in stark contrast to the gloomy paths her own thoughts were circling.

"I hope you're right."

This time when her eyelids slid closed, she allowed them to stay like that, lulled by his easy assurances.

Maybe because that's what she wanted to believe.

Either way, she found herself emptying her mind of anything that didn't revolve around the man beside her. And of how right, and good, and…restful it felt to be with him right now.

Dangerous to let him know that, though.

A hand squeezing hers brought her back. She blinked, the harsh glare of the overhead lights flooding her system.

Heavens, she'd fallen asleep. While her mom was undergoing bypass surgery.

"Jess, the doctor is heading this way."

She jerked her head off his shoulder so fast she thought it was going to bounce to the floor and roll down the hall. Dragging her attention to the present, she glanced past the wide door of the waiting room to see that her mom's doctor was indeed striding toward them, no longer wearing his scrubs.

Standing, she waited for him to reach her, vaguely aware that Clint had climbed to his feet beside her, his fingers at the small of her back as if knowing she still needed that connection.

Even before the doctor reached them, he flashed a thumbs-up sign and a smile. "Everything went really well, better than we could have hoped for, actually," he said. "The harvested vein went in without a hitch and her heart is going strong. She should feel better than she's felt in quite a while. Her other arteries still look pretty good. With a change in diet and exercise, hopefully they'll stay that way for a long time to come."

Relief rushed through her system. "So she's going to be okay?"

The doctor nodded. "Absolutely. Barring anything unforeseen, we'll release her in the next few days. She'll need someone home with her for about a week after that. We checked her insurance, and it'll cover a home nurse."

"Thank you so much. When can I see her?"

He smiled. "She's in Recovery at the moment. You know the routine. Once she's moved into a room, we'll let you see her." For the first time his glance slid smoothly to Clint. "But just you right now."

The touch at her back moved away.

Chelsea hurried to make the introductions, but left out why Clint was there, waiting with her.

The surgeon held out a hand. "Dr. Marks, good to meet you. I served as an army doc before moving over to private practice. I appreciate all you do for our military."

She tensed, wondering if Clint would question why he'd moved when there was so much need—much like she'd done when she'd heard about Dr. Cordoba resigning his commission. All Clint said, though, was, "I'm happy to do it. The country needs both civilian and military doctors. I'm glad you were there for Jessi's mom."

If Dr. Leonard thought it was strange that Clint was there with her or that he'd called her by her first name, he gave no hint of it. He simply nodded and let them know he'd send a nurse out to get Jessi when her mother was settled in. Then he turned around and headed back the way he'd come.

She glanced up at Clint. "Thanks for waiting with me. If you need to get back to the hospital, I understand."

"I already told you, I'm done for the day. I'll stay and make sure everything is okay."

"Thanks again." She bit the side of her lip. "Sorry for falling asleep on you. I can't believe I did that."

His fingers touched her back again. "You've been carrying a lot of weight around on those strong shoulders, Dr. Riley. Maybe it's time you let someone else help with the load from time to time."

Was he offering his services in that regard? And if he was, did she dare let him?

Maybe she already had just by accepting his offer to be here during the surgery.

"I'm sorry you've gotten dragged into my family's problems. Both in high school and now."

He turned her and laid his hands on her shoulders—

ignoring everyone else in the room. "No one 'dragged' me." He squeezed softly before letting her go. "Either then or now. I'm here because I want to be."

And later, after Chelsea was better. Would he still be there?

Something she didn't dare even think about at the moment. Because who knew when that would be. It could be years before Chelsea was well enough to function without the help of someone like Clint. Although she imagined the emphasis would be on counseling later, if there came a time that she didn't need medication to help her cope.

And Jessi knew how things worked in the military. Clint would be transferred out of here, either sooner or later, whereas she had settled her life in Richmond for the long haul. Her mom and daughter were here—not to mention Cooper—and she couldn't imagine leaving them.

Not even for Clint?

She stepped back a pace, not willing to face that question quite yet. Besides, there was nothing between them other than what boiled down to a couple of one-night stands.

One-night stands.

Why did that explanation make her throat ache in a way it hadn't all those years ago?

Hadn't it? Her subconscious whispered the question into her ear, but Jessi raised a hand and swished it away, making Clint frown.

"You okay?" he asked.

"Yes. Just relieved." She took another step back. "Seriously, you don't have to sit here with me. I'm sure you've got other things to do."

His frown grew deeper. "If you're worried about Chelsea or your mom finding out, don't. I won't tell them I was here unless you want me to."

"No!" She cleared her throat and lowered her voice

when she realized a couple of pairs of eyes in the waiting room had shifted their way. "I don't want to have to explain why."

Because she wasn't even sure of the answer, and she was afraid to look too closely at the possibilities. She might just discover something she was better off not knowing.

She'd already had her heart broken. Not once. But twice. Once by Clint and once by her husband's accusations. She didn't want to risk another crack in an already fragile organ.

Clint's voice was also low when he responded. "I already said I wouldn't say anything. So don't worry about it."

But he sounded a little less confident than he had a few minutes ago, when he'd assured her that her mother would be just fine.

"Thanks."

They both sat down, but this time without talking, and Clint didn't put his arm back around her. She tried to tell herself she was glad. But deep inside it made her feel lonely, yearning for something she was never going to have.

And what was that exactly?

A relationship with Clint?

Those four words caused a shudder to ripple through her. Her arms went around her waist, even though the waiting room wasn't chilly.

God, she hoped that's not what she was looking for. Because that wasn't on the cards for her or for Clint. Going down that road would be a recipe for disaster.

She would do better on that front, starting now. Despite her earlier thoughts, she needed to start relying on Clint less than she currently was.

The problem was, Jessi honestly didn't know how she was going to back away when the time came.

Because that crack in her heart was just waiting for an excuse to widen. And she had a feeling it was already far too late to stop that from happening. The crowbar was there in hand, poised and ready.

Or maybe it wasn't her hand that wielded that power at all.

What if, in the end, Clint was the one to decide if her heart came apart in jagged pieces or remained intact?

When the nurse finally came down to tell her her mom was awake and ready to see her, Jessi was relieved to be able to walk away from her spinning, panicked thoughts… and to put her attention firmly where it should have been all along: on her mom and Chelsea…and off Clint.

CHAPTER FIFTEEN

THE SUN WAS peeking out from between heavy storm clouds. Both figuratively and literally. At least as far as Chelsea was concerned. A good omen.

Jessi's mom was home and recovering after her bypass surgery. Clint had seen Jessi in passing, but she had her hands full at the moment with her job, her mom and her daughter.

Which brought him back to the item on his desk.

Transfer papers.

Or rather a request to terminate his temporary assignment in Richmond and head back to Cali, where, from what he'd read on the internet that morning, all was sunny and bright. Not a cloud in sight.

And, hell, he could use a little more light right now to clear his head.

To sign or not to sign, that was the question.

No, it wasn't. He'd eventually put in that request. It was only a matter of time. And willpower.

Willpower he'd been sorely lacking in the past several weeks. To stay would be a mistake. Something he'd convinced himself of time and time again.

His presence here in Richmond brought back memories of not-so-happy times for all of them.

How many times had Jessi mentioned Larry's name?

Hell, he hadn't even known the man had died when he'd arrived here, much less the reason for it. And Jessi had been carrying that around for all these years.

And being here with her was a definite reminder of his own bitter childhood. People from his past knew more than he'd realized—judging from Mrs. Spencer's comments at dinner. They'd evidently talked amongst themselves about his father's problems.

And Clint's explosive reactions when he was around Jessi? Also reminders of what a lack of control could cause—had caused. He might have enjoyed it at the time, but there were consequences for everything in this life.

He'd have to leave some time or other. Why not now? Chelsea was scheduled to be released from the hospital next week. She'd continue her sessions as an outpatient... a victory he should be cheering, instead of acting like he was about to be shot off to the moon, never to be heard from again.

Maybe he'd request deployment instead. That should take him far enough away. Or he could just let the army decide where he was needed, rather than ask to return to San Diego.

Chelsea popped her head in, as if she'd heard his thoughts. "Have you heard anything about my grandmother yet?"

He slid the transfer papers beneath a file folder, not willing to let her see it. No need to cause a panic. It would take time for the orders to go through, anyway.

"No, just that she's been released." He smiled at her. "And you really should learn to knock, young lady. I could have been with a patient."

He motioned at the chair across from his desk.

Her lips twisted. "You're right. Sorry."

"No problem." He tapped the eraser end of his pencil on the smooth gray surface of the desk, the hidden papers glaring at him from their hiding place. "As I was saying, your grandmother seems to be doing pretty well, according to your mom. She just has to take it easy for a few weeks."

Just like he did. He'd seen firsthand the problems that jumping into something with both feet could bring.

"Hmm…"

"And what does that sound mean?" He forced a light smile, although it felt like the corners of his mouth were weighted down with chunks of concrete.

Chelsea's own light attitude vanished. "I was hoping to do something, but I guess it can wait until Nana's feeling better."

"Anything I can help with?"

"I'm not sure. Maybe. I was telling Paul that I'd like to hold a memorial service for my…for the baby. He said he'd like to come. So did some of the others in our group."

Paul Ivers, a young man who'd moved over to sit by Chelsea during one of their group sessions. When had this particular conversation taken place?

"I don't see why that couldn't happen at some point."

"I'd want you there as well, if that's okay. You've helped me so much."

"I haven't done anything, Chelsea. You've come this far under your own power. I've just been here to listen and facilitate."

"Maybe you don't think you've done much, but I do. And you said you knew each other before. I asked Mom about that, and she said you, she and my dad were all in school together. My dad's not here anymore, so it would mean a lot if someone who knew him came."

Me and Larry, neck and neck.

He'd been a stand-in for the man back then. The last thing he wanted was to be one now.

Was that what he'd been when he'd made love to Jessi

back at her house? A stand-in for a man who was dead and gone? A man whose death he'd helped cause?

"Please, Dr. Marks?" Chelsea's voice came back again.

Clint sat there, conflicted. He believed in keeping his word whenever possible, something his father had never seen fit to do.

In fact, a lot of the strict rules governing his life had come about because of his dad's poor judgment. Maybe that wasn't such a bad thing. Those rules had served him well, until he'd come back to Richmond. "I can't promise anything, Chelsea, but if I'm still here, I'd love to come."

Her eyes widened then darkened with fear. "You're thinking of leaving?"

He hurried to put her mind at ease. "I simply meant if you hold the service five years from now, there are no guarantees I won't have been transferred somewhere else by then."

His buzzer went off before he had time to think.

When he answered, his assistant said, "Mrs. Riley is here."

His already tense muscles tightened further. Hearing Jessi referred to as Mrs. anything stuck in his craw.

Jessi Marks. Now, that had a nice ring to it.

No, it didn't.

Hell. This day was turning out to be anything but the good omen he'd hoped for fifteen minutes earlier. It was morphing into a damned nightmare.

"Oh, good," said Chelsea. "We can ask her what she thinks."

Perfect. He had a feeling Jessi was going to love this almost as much as he did.

He responded to his assistant, rather than to his patient. "Send her in."

Jessi scooted through the door, her face turning pink when she spied her daughter sitting in one of the chairs.

Then her eyes crinkled in the corners. "Hi, sweetheart. I was just headed down to see you."

"Were you?" Chelsea's lips slid into a smile. "Guess you decided to stop by and see my doctor first."

Pink turned to bright red that swept up high cheekbones like twin beacons of guilt.

Chelsea waved away her mother's discomfiture and stood up to catch her hand. "Anyway, I'm glad you did, because we have something to tell you."

"We do?"

"You do?"

He and Jessi both spoke at once, then their eyes met. Hers faintly accusing as she met him stare for stare. She was the first to look away, though.

Chelsea blinked as she glanced from one to the other. "I don't actually mean 'we' because I kind of sprang this on Dr. Marks."

That was one way of putting it.

She glanced at him again. "Is it okay if I tell her?"

"That's completely up to you." He had to force the words out as invisible walls began to close in around him. So much for his quick, silent escape. What a damn mess. No matter which way he spun, seeking the nearest exit, he only dug himself in deeper and deeper.

Pulling her mom over to the chairs, they both sat down, then Chelsea told Jessi what she'd told him, in almost exactly the same way. As if she'd been rehearsing the words over and over until she'd got them perfect.

His insides coiled tighter.

Once her voice died away there was silence in the room, except for Clint's phone, which gave a faint pinging sound as it received a message of some type.

Jessi licked her lips, her gaze flicking to Clint for a mere second before going to rest on her daughter. "I think that's a lovely idea."

"I asked Dr. Marks about letting the group come…and I invited him, as well. He said he'd be there, if he was still in Richmond."

"'Still in Richmond'?"

The words curled around a note of hurt, the sound splashing over him in a bitter wave.

This wasn't how he'd wanted her to hear the news.

Chelsea's hand covered her mother's. "No, I mean he said that if I had the service five years from now, he might have been transferred somewhere else by then."

Jessi's body relaxed slightly.

Did she care that he might move away?

Of course not. She had to know as well as he did how utterly foolish it would be for them to go any further than they already had. And she'd withdrawn a little over the past week, changing their working relationship into one of professionals who were collaborating on a patient they had in common. Only to Jessi she was no patient. She was her daughter—someone she loved with all her heart and soul. He saw the truth of it each time the women looked at each other and in the way Chelsea touched her mom, as if needing the reassurance of her presence.

To be loved like that would be…

Impossible. For him, anyway.

And he needed to pull himself together before someone realized how jumbled his emotions had become.

"Of course I'll be there." The words came out before he had time to fully vet them. So he added, "If I can."

"When do you want to do this?" Jessi's voice became stronger, as if she saw this as a way for her daughter to close this chapter in her life and move on to the next one. One that Clint hoped with all his being would be full of laughter and happiness. This family deserved nothing less, they'd been through so much over the years.

He did not need to add more junk to the pile. They both

had enough to deal with right now. He decided to change the subject. "How's your mom?"

"Good. The home nurse is with her this morning. She's getting stronger every day. In fact, she said today that finding out…er…finding out about her blockage might have been one of the most positive, life-affirming experiences she'd ever gone through. She feels tons better and is raring to get out of bed and go back to work on her garden and play with Cooper." Jessi shook her head and squeezed Chelsea's hand. "I think I know where you got your stubbornness from."

"Mine?"

Laughing, Jessi said, "Okay, mine, too."

That was one thing Clint could attest to. This was one strong trio of women, despite the momentary flashes of pain that manifested themselves in physical reactions: Abigail's heart blockage. Chelsea's suicide attempt. Jessi's reaching out to an old flame during a crisis?

Yes. That was exactly it.

It should have made him feel better—set his mind at ease about leaving in the months ahead. Instead, a cold draft slid through his body and circled, looking for a place to land. He cleared his throat to chase it away. It didn't work. It lay over him in a gray haze that clung to everything in sight, just like the morning dew. What it touched, it marked.

And that mark was…

Love.

He reeled back in his seat for a second, trying to process and conceal all at the same time.

He loved her? Heaven help him.

How could he have let this happen? Any of it? All of it?

He had screwed up badly. Had let his emotions get the best of him, just like he always had when he was around this woman.

The transfer papers seemed to pulse at him from beneath the binder with new urgency. The sooner he did this the better.

And his promise to Chelsea?

"What do you think Nana would want me to do?" Even as his own thoughts were in shambles, Chelsea's were on the brink of closing old wounds and letting them heal.

"I think Nana would want you to be happy, honey."

"Can we have the service next week, then? I don't know how long the members of the group will keep coming to sessions. We can have a private memorial for just our family later, if Nana feels up to it."

"We can have it anytime you want."

And in that moment he knew he had to see this through. He had to be there for Jessi, just as she had to be there for Chelsea. Abigail wasn't up to taking on that role yet. And Larry was no longer there.

And he wanted to. Wasn't that what love was about? Sacrificing your own comfort and well-being for someone else's?

Like he'd done once upon a time?

He peered into the past with new eyes. Eyes that saw the truth.

He'd loved her even then. Even as he'd been preparing to hand her over to another man. One whose father didn't drink himself into a rage and let his fists do the talking.

A normal, mundane life.

Something Clint hadn't been able to give her. Because back then he'd had anger issues, too. Toward his father, who'd dished it out. Toward his mom, who'd sat there and taken it. Toward the world in general, for turning a blind eye toward what had been going on in homes like his.

The military had helped him conquer most of his anger, but only because it had instilled discipline in its place, and had channeled his negative energy into positive areas.

But his life still wasn't peaceful. It was filled with patients like Chelsea, who scrabbled and clawed to find some kind of normalcy.

Jessi had been through enough. She'd deserved better than him back then, and she still did today.

She deserved a professor or architect or poet. A man who brought beauty into her life. Not memories of days gone by.

I'm going to have to give her up all over again.

And he was going to have a few more scars to show for it.

He realized both pairs of female eyes were on his face, both wearing identical expressions of confusion. One of them had said something.

"I'm sorry?"

Chelsea bit her lip. "I asked if next Sunday would work for you? Or do you have other plans?"

"No. No plans." Once he'd said it, he realized he could have come up with an excuse. Like what? A date? That would go over really well with Jessi. Besides, he'd meant what he'd thought earlier. He wanted to be there for her... and for Chelsea. Like the family he'd never had?

Maybe. Maybe it was okay to pretend just for a few hours—to soak up something he'd never be able to have in real life.

Like a wife and daughter?

Yes.

Even if they both belonged to a man who could no longer be there for them.

So he would act as a stand-in once again. For an hour. Maybe two. And he could pray that somehow it was enough to get him through the rest of his life.

CHAPTER SIXTEEN

She wanted to hold Clint's hand, but she couldn't.

Not in a cemetery, while mourning a tiny life that had been snuffed out before its time. Standing next to him would have to be enough.

Only it was so hard. Hard to remain there without touching him.

Curling her fingers into her palms, she forced them to stay by her sides as a chaplain she'd never met talked about life and death…commemorating a granddaughter she'd also never met.

A hand touched hers. Not Clint's, but Chelsea's. Her daughter's fingers were icy cold, her expression grim, eyes moist with grief as the minister continued to speak.

"In the same way this marker serves as a reminder that a tiny life was placed into Your loving arms, we, like Marie Elizabeth Riley, need to place our trust and hope in You, the Author and Finisher of our faith, that we will one day see her as she was meant to be. Whole and full of life…"

The sudden rush of tears to eyes that had been dry took Jessi by surprise, overriding whatever else the chaplain was saying. She fumbled in her purse, letting go of Chelsea's hand for a second as she searched for a tissue.

Clint, still, solemn and heartbreakingly handsome in a dark blue suit, pressed a handkerchief into her trembling hands. She glanced up at him to find him watching her, something dark and inscrutable in his gray eyes. Was he irritated at her for blubbering? But this baby would have been her first grandchild…would have probably survived if Chelsea had had access to health care.

And that was another thing that had driven her daughter crazy with guilt. All those what-ifs. *If* she had just spoken up…*if* she'd admitted she was pregnant, instead of fearing a reprimand or, worse, of being sent home in flurry of paperwork and inner shame…*if* she'd told her captors the truth. The baby's father had never been notified. Chelsea saw no reason to cause trouble for a man with whom she'd had a one-night stand.

Jessi knew what that was like. She'd had two of them. Both with the same man.

The chaplain asked everyone to bow their heads, so Jessi closed her eyes. And felt a hand to her right clasp hers once again. Chelsea.

And then, out of nowhere, warm fingers enveloped her other hand, lacing between hers.

Clint.

Oh, God. The tears flowed all over again. She'd wanted to hold his hand, and he'd not only read her mind, he'd found a way to accomplish the impossible.

A flicker of hope came to life in her chest.

Maybe it wasn't impossible. He had certainly made love to her like she'd meant something to him.

Then again, he'd done the same thing all those years ago. Maybe it was different now. They were both older. Wiser. They'd both lived through things many people never had to experience.

She tightened her grip around both hands, allowing herself to feel connected to him in a way that had nothing to do with sex. Or need. But was something deeper. More profound.

No.

Not happening.

And yet he'd made the impossible possible.

As the prayer went on, Clint gave her hand a quick squeeze, then released it.

When she peeked between her lashes, she saw that she wasn't the only one who had a male hand linked with hers. The young man next to Chelsea stood so close their shoulders and arms touched. And his index finger was twined around her daughter's.

She swallowed. Maybe, just maybe, she could let herself believe. Just like the chaplain said.

The seed took root and spread throughout her being, twisting around her heart and lungs until she wasn't sure where they started and the belief ended. Maybe that was the way it was meant to be.

She could talk to Clint. Somehow find out if he felt the same way. Surely he did. Otherwise why would he have held her hand?

Because she'd been crying? Maybe. That was why it was important to talk to him. And she would. Just as soon as the service was over, and she'd made sure her daughter was okay. Her mom was at home. They still hadn't told Chelsea about the circumstances behind the heart episode, and they'd both agreed to keep that quiet. Her mom also felt it was best for her to stay at home for this particular event. Neither of them wanted anything to mar the service. And although Jessi trusted Clint not to say anything, one of them could inadvertently let something slip without realizing it.

The prayer ended, and Chelsea took the white rose in her hand and gently kissed the bloom, then placed it across the bronze marker that had been set in the lush grass beside Larry's grave. Grass that hadn't needed to be turned up, since there was no body to bury this time. The back of

Jessi's throat burned. Larry would have loved his daughter. And his granddaughter, if he'd been able to see past his own hurt and pride. Two lives, needlessly lost.

But at least there was now a place where Chelsea could come and remember—along with a concrete bench that had been placed at the foot of the graves, a gift from her mother. She hoped they could come here each year and remember.

The service ended with a flautist from their church playing "Amazing Grace," the light, bright sound of the instrument giving the hymn a sense of hope and peace. It's what Chelsea had wanted, and as her daughter moved to stand beside the same young man as before, a quick glance was shared between the two of them. Jessi looked at him a little more closely. Surely it was a good thing that her daughter was beginning to look past the pain in her heart and see a future that was brimming with possibilities.

Like Jessi herself was?

When she gave Clint a sideways look, she saw that his attention was also on the pair. She could have sworn a flash of envy crossed his expression before disappearing. His gaze met hers, and he nodded to show her he had noticed, then he leaned close, his breath brushing across her ear as he murmured, "Try not to worry. Paul's a good man."

Words hung on the tip of her tongue, then spilled past her lips. "So are you, Clinton Marks."

His intake of breath was probably not audible to anyone except him, but even so he froze for several seconds at her comment, while his brain played it over and over in that same breathy little whisper.

She thought he was a good man?

Emotion swelled in his throat, and he forced himself to stand up straight before he did something rash right in front of her late husband's grave. Like crush her in his arms and kiss her like there was no tomorrow. Tell her that he loved her and would always be there for her.

As the last notes of the song died away, people began to filter out of the cemetery. Chelsea leaned over to Jessi and said, "I'll see you later on at Nana's?"

"I probably won't be there for a few hours, okay? There's something I need to do first," said Jess.

"Okay." The two women embraced for several long seconds then broke apart. Paul walked her daughter over to her car and held the door open, leaning over to tell her something before closing it.

"What do you have to do?" Clint asked.

If he was smart, he'd say his goodbyes right now before he got caught up in some kind of sentimental voyage that would end with him dragging her back to his place.

"I thought we might go back to my house for a little while."

He waited for her to tack a valid reason on to the end of that phrase. But she didn't. Instead, she simply waited for him to respond to the request. One that had come right on the heels of her other shocking comment.

He should end it right now. Cut her short before she could say anything else with a brusque, "Not a good idea and you know it."

Right. He could no more bring himself to say something like that than the moon could grow an oxygen-rich atmosphere. Or maybe it could, because right now he was having trouble catching his breath and his head felt like it was ready shut down.

He glanced back at the markers, Larry's name biting deep into his senses and grinding them into something he no longer recognized. Needing to get away before it took another chunk from him, he said, "Sounds good. Are you ready?"

"Do you want to follow me back?"

Honey, I'd follow you anywhere, if I could.

Maybe things weren't as dire as he'd painted them. Would it be so bad if he and Jessi somehow tried to make a go of things?

That paper on his desk came to mind. He could just tear it up and dump it in his waste can, and no one would be the wiser.

The thought grew as they walked to the parking lot together. With no one else around, Clint took her hand again, gripping it with an almost desperate sense of reverence. This woman did it for him. She met him right at his point of deepest need. And she had no idea.

And if she wanted to go back to her place and discuss Chelsea's case, he was going to be crushed with disappointment. Because he wanted her. In the past. Right now in the present. And in the days that stretched far into the future.

Whether or not any of that was possible was another matter. But maybe he shouldn't worry about leaping right to the end of this particular book. Maybe he should turn one page at a time and savor each moment as it came.

Because who knew how long anything in this life was going to last? Wasn't today a reminder of that?

He saw her to her car and smiled when he did the exact same thing young Paul had done. Opened her door for her and then leaned across it. Only instead of saying something, he kissed her. Right on the mouth. Right in the middle of a public parking lot.

And he didn't give a rip who saw him.

One page at a time. And he was loving the current chapter because, instead of a quick peck and retreat, Jessi's lips clung to his for several long seconds. When he finally forced himself to pull back, she gave him a brilliant smile. "I think we're on the same page."

A roll of shock swished through him. Coincidence.

It had to be. Unless Jessi had suddenly become a mind-reader.

Then again, he found it pretty damned hard to hide his feelings from this particular woman. They bubbled up and out before he could contain them. That's what had gotten him into trouble when they'd been in high school and again a couple of weeks ago. It was impossible to be near her and not want to touch her. Hold her. Make love to her.

He didn't respond to her words, just said, "I'll meet you at your house." Because if he was wrong, if she wasn't feeling the same deep-seated need that he was, he'd end up eating his words and feeling like a fool.

The fifteen-minute drive seemed to take forever, but finally she pulled into the driveway of her house. They got out of their cars and stared at each other for a minute before coming together.

Then he was reaching for her and dragging her into his arms, kissing her with a fervor he had no business feeling. But she kissed him back just as hard, her hands winding around his neck, going up on tiptoe so she could get closer.

Her tongue found his, leaving no doubt in his mind where her thoughts were headed. And that was fine by him, because his had been there for hours...weeks.

"Keys." His muttered words were met with a jingle, then he swept her up in his arms and strode to the front door. "Unlock it."

It gave him a thrill to note that her hands shook as she twisted around to do as he asked, because he knew his were trembling just as hard, along with every other part of his body. Half in anticipation of what was to come and half in fear that somehow it was all going to fall apart before they got inside...before he got the chance to strip her clothes from her body—in her bedroom this time—and drive her to the point of no return.

Because he was already there. There was no turning

back from the emotions that were throbbing to life within him. He couldn't bring himself to say them, so he would show her instead. With his mouth. With his hands.

With his heart.

And hope that somehow she'd be able to decipher their meaning.

He kicked the door closed, trying not to trip when Cooper suddenly appeared, barking wildly and winding around him. He let Jessi down long enough for her to let the dog out into the backyard before hauling her back up into his arms. This time he lifted her higher so that his mouth could slant back over hers, his fingers digging into the soft flesh of her thighs, her waist. Right on cue, her arms went back around his neck and she held on tight.

Clung as if she were drowning.

Well, so was he.

"Bedroom," he muttered against her mouth. Could he not get anything out other than one- and two-word sentences?

Evidently not.

And if she was going to stop this parade, she had the perfect opportunity to drag her lips from his and tell him to put her down, that they were going to sit on that long sofa and talk.

She didn't. "Down the hallway, first door on the right."

Then she was kissing him again, her eyes flickering shut even as his had to remain open to avoid tripping over furniture or running into a wall as he made his way down the hallway and arrived at her bedroom. He paused in the doorway and eyed the space, noting the frilly pillows on the bed and the hinged frame that held two pictures on the nightstand. One of Jessi with another man. And one of her holding that man's baby.

Larry.

His chest tightened, and he pulled back slightly, rethinking this idea.

"What's wrong?" Her breathless reply washed over him.

He nodded at the nightstand, and she glanced in that direction and then tensed before looking back up at him. She shook her head. "It's okay, Clint. He's been gone a very long time."

She didn't say that she didn't love him, or that Larry wouldn't mind if he could see them.

Just that the man had been gone a long time.

He stood there, undecided. Could he lie in that bed and thrust inside her, while her dead husband watched them?

"Take me over there," she murmured.

He didn't want to. Wanted to suggest they go back to the familiar sofa in the living room. But his feet had ideas of their own. He carried her over to the small table and watched as she tipped the frame over onto its front so that the pictures were no longer visible.

"Better?" she asked, one corner of her mouth curling.

It was. A little, anyway. "Yes."

"Okay, now put me on the bed—" her fingers sifted through the hair at the back of his neck, sending a shiver over him "—and take off all my clothes."

"Your wish—" he wiped Larry from his mind and dropped her from where he stood, then smiled at the squeal she gave as she bounced on the mattress and lay there staring up at him "—is my command."

She licked her lips. "Then come down here and start commanding me."

CHAPTER SEVENTEEN

BEFORE HE COULD do as she asked, Jessi sat up and scooted to the edge of the bed, allowing her legs to hit the floor. Then she grabbed him behind the knees and dragged him forward a step or two, parting her legs until he stood between them.

"I thought I was doing the commanding," he said.

"Changed my mind," she said with a laugh, removing his keys and wallet from his pockets and putting them on the bed. "Because you'll end up having all the fun, like last time."

His brows went up. "I don't remember hearing any complaints."

"That's because there weren't any." Reaching for his belt buckle, she slid the loop out in one smooth move that made his mouth water. "And I don't think you'll be hearing any complaints now. At least, not from me."

With the buckle undone, she moved to the button of his dress slacks.

Hell, she wasn't going to hear any complaints from him either. Although his ideas for maneuvering her to the point of no return were not going according to plan.

Or maybe she'd had the very same thoughts about him.

His flesh twitched.

And he was already too far gone to back out now.

Down went his zipper. "Wait."

She stopped and met his eyes. "Am I doing something wrong?"

No, she was doing everything exactly right. And that was the problem. He really *was* too far gone. His body was pumping with anticipation. Too much too soon and he was going to have trouble not letting go in a rush. It was why he hadn't let her touch him last time.

"No, honey." His hand tangled in her hair, resisting the urge to drag her forward and show her exactly what he meant. "I just don't want you to do anything you don't want to do."

One perfectly arched brow went up an inch, and she licked her lips. "And if I want to?"

Even as she said it, she peeled apart the edges of his slacks and pushed them down his hips, until they sat at midthigh.

No trying to hide what she did to him at this point, because it was right there in front of her. Her hands moved around to the backs of his thighs, sliding over his butt and grabbing the elastic waistband of his briefs. "Are you ready?"

Oh, he was ready all right. But he wasn't so sure he was ready for what she wanted.

Dammit, who was he kidding? He was a man. He wanted it. Wanted every last thing she could think of doing to him.

And he wanted it now.

"Do it."

That was all it took. She dragged his underwear down in one quick tug, her nails scraping over his butt in a sensual move that set all his nerve endings on high alert.

He bobbed free, inches from her face. Her thumbs brushed along the outsides of his legs as her hands curled around the backs of his thighs, holding him in place. Then she leaned forward without hesitation, her mouth engulfing him in a hot, wet rush that made him grunt with ecstasy.

She remained like that for several seconds, completely still, her eyes closed, nostrils flaring as if the sensation was heavenly.

Hell, lady, you should be standing in my shoes.

He struggled like a wild man to contain the warning tingle, using every bit of ammunition in his bag of tricks to keep from erupting right then and there. Tangling his hand in her hair, he dragged her backward until he popped free. "Damn, woman. You're going to get more than you bargained for if you keep that up."

She laughed. "Haven't I told you? I love bargains. Especially when I get more bang for my…buck."

The pointed hesitation before she said that last word made his flesh tighten in anticipation. A silent promise to give her exactly what she wanted: a hard, fast bang that was, oh, so good.

Just like last time.

But this time he wanted to draw out his pleasure. And hers.

So, keeping his fingers buried in her hair, he drew her forward again, watching as she slowly opened her mouth.

Yes!

He edged closer, dying to feel her on him, then pulled away at the last second. He repeated the parry and feint several times with a slow undulation of hips that was a blending of obscene torture—emphasis on the torture. At least for him.

She clenched the backs of his thighs, trying to tug him closer, while he remained just out of reach. "Clint. Please…"

"What do you want, Jess?"

"Right now? I want you."

That was all it took. He pushed her backwards on the

bed, knocking the frame off the end table in the process, and shoved her full skirt up around her hips. Black satin panties met his hungry eyes. He jerked them down and then kicked his way out of the rest of his clothes, cursing when one foot got hung up in the waistband of his briefs. Once free, he tossed a condom packet onto the bed and lay down, hauling her on top of him, until she was straddling him, her skirt pooling around her hips.

"You wanted to be in control, Jess? You've got it."

Her eyes trailed from the straining flesh outlined beneath the fabric of her skirt up his bare chest, until her eyes met his. "In that case, do you want me clothed? Or unclothed?"

Unclothed. His mind screamed the word, mouth going dry. He had to force himself to say, "Your game. Your rules."

She gave him a slow smile. "Mmm. I like the idea of making my own rules." Taking her skirt in hand, she pulled the black silk up his erection in a long, slow move that made him rethink his assessment. Then she let it slip back down the way it had come.

Okay, clothed was pretty hot, too. Especially when she continued to hold his gaze, and he knew she could spot every muscle twitch in his cheek, discern every time he had to hold himself in check. Like now, when myriad sensations began to gather in his chest. In his gut...

"Jess..." It was meant to be a warning, but her name came out as a low hum of air.

One of her hands crawled beneath her skirt and found him. And the tactile awareness of being able to feel what she was doing but not see it made the act seem secretive and forbidden. An exotic ritual that defied time and space.

She slid forward and shifted her hips up and over his ready flesh. He braced himself, but she didn't come down on him in a rush, as he'd expected. Instead, she brushed him across her skin, back and forth, her eyes closing, lips parting. He swallowed hard when he realized what she was doing—using him on her body, giving herself pleasure, rocking her hips in time with her hand.

Holy hell. This was as hot as her mouth had been.

Worse.

Because then she'd only been pleasuring him. Now she was bringing both of them to new heights of throbbing awareness. Every cell in his body wanted to thrust home and end the torment. He could just slide up and inside her in one fast move, and she would probably let him... probably welcome him. But the shifting expressions on her face were too entrancing to do anything but lie there and take whatever she wanted to dish out.

"God, Jess. You're killing me here."

"What do you want?" She turned his earlier words around and pushed them back at him.

Only he knew exactly what he wanted. "I want you to make yourself come."

Her fingers tightened, and her movements became quicker, bolder, her breasts straining beneath her shirt as she brushed herself against him—or brushed him against herself—he didn't know which it was and didn't care. He was dying to cup her, to scrape his thumb across those hard nipples now visible even through her blouse and bra, but he wanted this round to be all hers.

All around him, he felt her slick heat. Lust spiraled through him, growing stronger with each stroke, even as her movements became more purposeful. Reaching sideways, Clint found his wallet and the condom just inside it. He wrapped his fingers around the plastic wrapper, gripping it tight, hoping he'd still have the sanity to use it when the time came.

Jessi's breathing quickened, her teeth coming down on her lip as her body continued to feign the motions of sex.

Good sex. The kind of sex that didn't come along every day, with every woman.

No, there was only one woman he'd ever shared this kind of connection with.

Her body stiffened suddenly, pressing hard against him. Then she went off with a cry, her body pulsing against the tight need of his erection. Tearing into the packet, he reached beneath her skirt and sheathed himself in a rush before plunging into her and losing himself in the continued contractions of her orgasm.

Using her hips, he pulled her down onto himself as hard as he could, already too far gone to try to last any longer. Instead, he pressed upwards in greedy thrusting motions as he allowed himself to plummet mindlessly over the cliff of his own release, falling, falling, until there was nowhere else to go.

Nothing registered for several seconds—or it might have been minutes. Hours, even.

When he could finally breathe again, finally think, he gathered her to his chest, his fingers sliding up through the damp strands of her hair and holding her close.

"Remind me not to put you in charge ever again."

"So you *are* complaining." She snuggled closer.

"Never."

He kissed her brow, her taste salty with perspiration, and allowed his eyelids to finally swing shut...no longer afraid he was going to miss something crucial.

With one last sigh, he propped his chin on her head and allowed his body to relax completely.

Something tickled the side of her arm.

There it was again. It wasn't Cooper, because he was in the living room, and the bedroom door was shut.

Her mind reached out to grasp something, only to have

it shift away uneasily. The sensation returned. A light rhythmic stroke trailing up toward her shoulder now.

Her eyes opened to find someone standing beside the bed, watching her.

Clint.

"Hello, sleepyhead. I fed Cooper and let him out. Hope that was okay."

"Mmm..."

Since his voice sounded as rough as hers felt, she wasn't the only one who had fallen asleep after the second time they'd made love.

In her bed. In her house. And the second time he'd undressed her slowly. Carefully. Kissing his way down her body in a way that had made her heart melt, even while her senses had been kicking into high gear.

Like now. Only it was her heart that was soaring, rather than her libido. Because Clint was still here. He hadn't hightailed it out of here like she'd half expected. The hope she'd grasped earlier continued to grow, picking up speed as she finally acknowledged the possibilities that this might just work out between them.

"Hey, yourself. What time is it?" She rolled onto her back to look at him fully.

"About five in the afternoon." A hand reached up to scrub the stubble on his jaw. "Do you have to work?"

Work? At a time like this?

"Have you been walking around the house like that?" The man had fed Cooper and let him out...stark naked?

He smiled. "Why? Does it bother you?"

"Define bother."

He laughed. "So, about work..."

"No. No work, but I need to check on Chelsea and my mom, like I told them I would."

"I thought you might. Otherwise I would have let you sleep. As it was, if Cooper hadn't scratched at the door, I was going to wake you in a completely different way." He found one of her hands and linked his fingers through hers.

She closed her eyes, happiness flowing over her. "Wow. You're up for a third round?"

"Believe me, I'm up for all kinds of things. Round or otherwise." A quick glance down showed he was already up and ready.

"Mmm." She let out a sigh as a thought came to her. Talk. That's what she'd meant to do at some point, only she'd gotten sidetracked. She dipped a toe into the water. "Do you think Chelsea and Paul are going to start seeing each other?"

"I think it's a possibility. Why? Is that a problem?"

"Do you think it's a good idea?"

"Don't know. They've both been through some tough times. They'll either be able to support each other, or they'll drag each other down."

A shiver went over her. "I hope I never have to live through anything like the past couple of months ever again. How do you deal with patients who are in such pain on a daily basis? I think it would eat at my heart." She hesitated before continuing. "And after what happened with your dad…"

Lifting his hand to kiss it, his crooked little finger caught her attention. She changed her aim and kissed that knuckle instead.

He stiffened at her act. "My dad is the reason I'm in this line of work."

Pulling away, he reached down and picked something up off the floor. She frowned, and then saw it was the picture frame he'd knocked off. Flipping it over, he went to put it on the nightstand then stopped, his jaw tightening as he stared at it.

"Clint?"

He shook his head, throat moving for a second. Jessi swiveled her eyes to look at the frame.

The glass on Larry's side had broken, a series of jagged, cobweb-looking cracks distorting his features and obscuring half of his face.

When she glanced back at Clint he looked…stricken. That was the only word she could think to describe it.

She reached out a hand. "Hey, it's okay. It's only a cheap frame. I can get another one."

He set it on the table but wouldn't quite meet her eyes.

Something was wrong. Very wrong.

"Jessi, I need to tell you something."

A wave of foreboding licked at her toes, then her ankles. Soon it was waist deep and rising.

She reached out to touch him, but the second she did, he backed away and found his trousers, sliding into them and fastening them before he looked at her again.

"I was going to wait and tell you later, but this seems as good a time as any." A muscle worked in his jaw. "They've found a permanent replacement for Dr. Cordoba. He arrives in two weeks."

She wasn't sure what this had to do with them. "Chelsea will continue her sessions with him, then."

"Yes." He scooped his dress shirt from the floor and pushed his arms through the sleeves.

Why was he getting dressed? This was good news. They wouldn't have to hide their relationship anymore.

Right?

"So that means we'll be able to see each other without—"

"No." His lean fingers moved quickly to button up his shirt. "We won't. I'm putting in my transfer papers. You knew this was only a temporary assignment. Just until they found another doctor. I'm going back to San Diego."

What? Her mind screamed that word over and over and over until it was hoarse with grief and confusion.

He'd made love to her last night as if he couldn't get enough. As if she really meant something to him. And now he was leaving?

Shades of the past came back to haunt her. Hadn't he already done this once before? Screwed her and then taken off without a backward glance?

The ominous wave was still rising, faster than ever, splashing up her neck and cresting over her head until she couldn't breathe. Horror washed through her at all she'd done with him last night, at how truly and freely she'd given herself to him.

In. Love.

And he'd felt nothing. *Nothing.*

As the silence drew out, he finally broke it by saying, "I should have told you before…" He motioned at the bed.

He hadn't been willing to change his life for her twenty-odd years ago so why had she thought he would now?

Sitting up and not bothering to cover her nakedness, she glared at him, welcoming the anger—because it kept away the tears. "Yes, you should have. But, then, you wouldn't have had one last trip down memory lane, would you? Treating patients isn't the only thing you're good at, Dr. Marks. You're also an expert at using people, and then ditching them when you've had what you wanted."

She climbed to her feet and stood there. Refusing to be vulnerable. Refusing to care what he did.

Only she knew deep inside it was a lie. The cracks in the picture frame now mirrored the ones in her heart, splitting wide open and spilling everything inside her into the dust that had become her life.

"Jess, that's not the way this—"

"No!" If he said one more word she was either going to burst into tears or slap him across the face with all her might. "Just go. Have Chelsea's new doctor call us when he arrives."

He grabbed the rest of his clothes and shoved his bare feet into his dress shoes. "I'm sorry, Jess."

Tossing her head, she bit out a quick reply. "Don't be. It was a blast from the past. We had our own mini high school reunion right here in my bedroom, but now it's time to pack up and get back to our own lives, in our own cities."

She didn't ask him exactly when he was leaving. She didn't want to know.

Clint's throat moved as he looked at her for another minute. Then he said, "Goodbye, Jessi."

With that, he turned around and walked out of the bedroom, his receding footsteps on the hardwood floor marking his location and searing the message into her brain. There was no slowing of his pace, no hesitation as the front door opened and then closed.

Clint was leaving. And this time he wasn't coming back.

CHAPTER EIGHTEEN

A WEEK WAS all it took to change his life forever.

He'd filed expedited transfer papers, asking them to put him wherever they needed him, preferably deployed overseas. He wound up at the VA hospital in New Mexico instead.

It might as well have been the other side of the world.

He sat at a desk that looked exactly like his previous one and wondered how he'd gotten here. Aimless. Rootless. And, thus far, patientless. They were letting him get settled in.

Right. Like that's what he needed. More time to think about what had happened that night in Jessi's bedroom.

He'd been all set to tell her how he felt, and then he'd picked up that frame and seen the damage he'd caused.

To her marriage. To her life.

At that moment he'd felt as shattered as that glass.

Being with Jessi again had wreaked havoc with his insides, turning him back into that impulsive screwup he'd been in high school.

He couldn't risk messing up her life a second time. Neither could he ask her to pick up and move away the next time he got his transfer papers. Jessi's life was in Richmond. With Chelsea and her mom—and those two graves.

Clint's place was with his patients. The one thing he knew he was good at.

She'd be okay without him. Seeing Chelsea get better would give her hope for a new beginning. He'd soon be relegated to the past again—where he belonged.

His phone rang. He glanced at the readout and his mouth went dry, his blood pressure spiking.

A Richmond area code.

Only it wasn't Jessi's number. He didn't recognize it.

Damn it!

When would the hope finally die? It was over. He'd ended it himself—and she hadn't been sorry to see him go. She'd not said one word to discourage him. Instead, she'd practically shoved him out the door.

Checking the door to his office to make sure it was closed, he pressed the speakerphone button and stared at the open case file in front of him. So much for trying to get up to speed.

"Hello?"

"Dr. Marks?"

He recognized the voice immediately. "Chelsea? Is everything okay?"

"I don't know. I mean, everything's fine with me. It's Mom."

His heart plummeted. "Is she all right?"

"No." There was a pause, and then her voice came through. Stronger. With just a hint of accusation. "I saw you holding hands at the memorial service. How could you just…leave like that?"

"I was transferred. You know how it works."

A curse word split the air, and Clint picked the phone up and put it to his ear, even though he knew his assistant wouldn't be able to hear their conversation through the thick walls.

Chelsea's voice came back through. "You're right. I do

know how it works. And there's no way you'd be able to get the okay for a transfer that fast unless you asked for it to be expedited. Or unless you'd been sitting on it this whole time."

"What does it matter? The Richmond hospital was a temporary assignment."

"Did I say something? Do something?"

"No." He hurried to set her mind at ease. "This had nothing to do with you, Chelsea. I'm proud of how hard you've worked on your recovery. You've faced the past head-on and now you're ready to move into the future."

A laugh came over the phone, but it was without humor. "That's what you always told us during group, wasn't it? That we had to face the past and see it for what it was without running or hiding from the truth. But in the end that's not what you did, is it?"

Hell, how had a tiny slip of a girl managed to read him so well? He had run. He'd taken one look at that broken glass, and instead of facing his fears, instead of talking to Jessi about everything that had happened, he'd turned tail and run.

Because he was afraid to face the future. Afraid his past would somehow catch up to him and splash its ugliness on to Jessi.

In reality, he'd been looking for an excuse to flee ever since he'd seen her sitting in his office that first day.

Why? Because he loved her, and just like back in high school he'd hightailed it out of town rather than having the courage to tell her how he felt and let her decide what to do with that information.

"What happened between me and your mother isn't any of your business."

"Sure it is. She's. My. Mother." She took an audible breath. "When I was in trouble, you never hesitated to bleed every detail of my therapy to her, because…she had a right to know the truth. She's listed as my next of kin. Well, guess what, Doctor, that works both ways. I'm her next of kin. I have a right to know. Did you even care about her at all?"

He swallowed. "Yes."

"Well, she cares for you, too. She's been smiling and saying all the right things, but she's not okay. She looks awful."

"I'm sorry."

"Not good enough. You might outrank me, but I'm going to tell you straight up what I think."

He smiled despite himself. "There's no question you and your mom are related."

"Yeah? Well, here it is. You're no better than a common deserter."

Shock rolled through him. "Excuse me?"

"You heard me. When the battle inside your head got tough, you turned around and walked away, instead of acting like a soldier and facing it, the way you told us to do. She's not the enemy, Dr. Marks. I don't know what it is you're fighting, but I suggest you figure it out and come back and face it. Otherwise you'll regret it for the rest of your life."

She looks awful.

He'd rushed off so sure that he was doing the right thing and saving the woman he loved a whole lot of pain.

What if he'd ended up *causing* her pain instead?

Hell. He was an idiot. "Reprimand noted and accepted."

"Good. You said you cared about her. Do you love her?"

He smiled, making a decision he should have made twenty-two years ago. "I think your mom deserves to hear that from the source, don't you?"

"Then get back here and tell her. Because I'm pretty sure she loves you, too."

* * *

Jessi pulled her sticky scrubs away from her midsection, fanning the fabric against herself as she headed into the parking lot. It was an hour past the end of her shift, and she was only now able to leave the hospital.

A gang war had seen her dealing with multiple gunshot wounds. Two had died en route to the hospital and another three had needed surgery. One of them had a broken finger in addition to other more serious wounds, but that small injury had been the one that had made her finally break down and admit the truth. That she missed Clint. Terribly.

She had a feeling Chelsea knew something was wrong, and her mom—almost completely recovered from her surgery a month ago—had also cast some worried looks her way. She had no idea why. She'd been acting cheerful, even if that's all it was. An act.

Straightening her back, she quickened her pace. This was ridiculous. How long was she going to keep mooning over something that was never going to happen? She needed to pull herself together and forget about…

Keys in hand, she paused halfway across the parking lot. Someone in uniform stood near where she'd parked her car, the tall military bearing painfully familiar. How many times had she seen that stance?

Her dad. Her daughter. In a military town, it was impossible not to recognize the proud upright posture. Only this went beyond that. This was…

Clint.

Oh, God. Something inside her urged her to turn around and dash back to the safety of the hospital.

No. She was not going to let what that man did or didn't do dictate her actions and emotions any longer. So she walked toward him, trying not to look directly at him as she did so, afraid he'd see the misery in her eyes.

When she reached her car she saw that she was right, he was standing right next to it. She'd have to pass in front of him to get to the driver's door.

"I thought you'd left," she said, her voice sounding as chipper as ever.

"I did." He didn't move. Didn't crack a smile at her tone. "I came back."

Her heart took a swan dive. What? Had he decided he hadn't tortured her enough?

She swallowed. "Why?"

"Because I'm done running. When you told me about Larry and his death, it was like a hole opened up and swallowed me whole. If I hadn't followed you that day...if I'd let him chase you outside instead, you'd still be one big happy family."

He drew in an audible breath. "And then I broke that frame, Larry's frame, and it was as if the universe was sending me a message. That I'd screwed up your life once before, and I could very well do it again if I stayed."

Her own breath caught in her lungs before whooshing back out. "Why didn't you say something?"

"I thought I was doing you a favor."

"Well, you didn't. I——" He cut her off with a finger pressed across her lips.

"Let me finish, while I still have the nerve. I came back to tell you I love you. I have since high school when I found you crying beside the creek." He paused. "I gave you up once, thinking it was for your own good, but I'm not going to do it again. Unless you tell me to go."

She pushed his hand away.

"Twice." The correction came out before she could stop it. "You gave me up twice. Why should I believe you this time?"

"Because it's the truth, Jess. I swear it." He took a step forward.

She tried to force herself to move back, but she couldn't. She just stood there, staring up at him. Maybe the summer heat had gone to her head and he was a mirage. After all, he didn't look hot at all.

Okay, so he looked superhot in that uniform, but not in the way she'd meant it.

"So what changed your mind this time?"

She had to know he hadn't just come back on a whim. That he was here for the long haul this time.

"That's a complicated question. I've never been truly terrified of anything—not even my father. But you scare me, Jess. The fear that I might not be good enough for you because of my past. Larry's death just seemed to echo that fear. It took a wise young woman to set me straight."

She frowned, until something clicked. "Chelsea."

He nodded. "Yes. She challenged me to come back and face my fears. So here I am. This is my battleground, and I'm not going to retreat. Not this time. Unless you tell me to."

He was handing her the power. Just like the last time they made love. Only this time it wasn't a game, and she had to be very sure of her heart. Trust that he wasn't going to leave, this time. That he wasn't going to take off like Larry and do something crazy, instead of sitting down and talking out their problems.

Did she trust him?

Yes. If he had the guts to face his fears, then she owed it to herself—and him—to do the same.

"Well, I guess we're at an impasse, then," she said in as serious a voice as she could manage, when all she wanted to do was throw herself into his arms and kiss him until neither of them could breathe. "Because I'm not going to tell you to leave. And you're evidently not going to leave on your own."

His eyes clouded for a second, but he stood firm. "No, I'm not."

"Then you'll just have to stay." She thought of something. "Wait. What about your transfer?"

"It hasn't been officially approved, it was still in the works, but they let me move early. My current contract is almost up, so I can resign my commission—go into private practice—if that tilts the odds in my favor. We wouldn't have to move. Ever. We could stay right here in Richmond."

This time she did throw herself at him, wrapping her arms around his neck. "Those odds were already tilted once I saw you standing here. I love you, too, Clint, no matter what you decide to do. You do so much good for people like Chelsea. And if the paperwork on your transfer goes through before you can cancel it, I'm coming with you."

He grabbed her up and held her tight—so tight that she felt the air rush from her lungs. She didn't care.

She loved this man. More than she ever had.

Leaning down, he caught her mouth in a kiss that held a wealth of love and longing. "There's only one thing I want to do right now."

She laughed. "Really? Can it wait until I've had something to eat?"

"It could, but…" He withdrew and reached inside the jacket of his uniform, pulling out a small jeweler's box.

Her hands went over her mouth, afraid the sun and heat were still playing tricks on her. "Clint?"

He snapped the box open to reveal a ring. Small and twinkling and perfect. "It was my grandmother's. Mom gave it to me before I went into the service. She said I might need it one day. She was right." He smiled. "I'd get down on one knee, but I'm afraid I'd be seared permanently to the pavement if I did. Damn, I'm screwing this all up. I should have waited to ask you to marry me until dinner, when we could have champagne, or until I had the ring resized—"

"No. This is the perfect place. The perfect ring. And you're the perfect man for me." Tears gathered in her eyes. "And I accept your proposal, Colonel Clinton Marks."

He kissed her again. Then Jessi unhooked the chain from her necklace and let him slide the slender ring onto it, where it dangled in the hollow of her collarbone. Fingering it while heat waves danced over the black tar surface of the parking lot, she blinked. "Where's your car?"

"Someone offered me a lift."

She could guess who that might be. "Chelsea again?"

"Yes."

"So you've been standing in the parking lot for over an hour?"

"Not quite. I had a little help tracking your movements."

Ahh…so that's why Chelsea's text—asking her to let her know the second she got off work—had been waiting for her when she'd switched her phone back on.

She clicked the button to unlock her car. "I guess we should put her out of her misery, then."

"Already done. I told her if you weren't home in an hour to assume we were out celebrating somewhere."

"Oh? You were that sure of yourself, were you?"

He grinned. "You have no idea what I've been through over the past month. I wasn't sure of anything, least of all myself."

"So what kind of celebration were you thinking of?"

He slid into the passenger seat and waited for her to join him. "I was thinking of something small and private."

"Interesting." Her pulse rate sped up, despite her earlier words about eating something. "So whose turn is it to be in charge this time?"

He eased his fingers deep into her hair and turned her

face toward him. "How about if from now on we make sure it's an equal partnership?"

"Yes," she breathed as he leaned down to kiss her again, allowing her senses to begin that familiar climb. "That's the perfect solution."

EPILOGUE

"Do you, Jessica Marie Riley, take Clinton Shane Marks to be your lawfully wedded husband?"

Clint faced Jessi as she said the words that would legally bind her to him. Only they were already bound by cords much stronger than anything the minister could say.

Jessi had convinced him that the broken frame didn't represent what he'd done to her life all those years ago. Instead, it symbolized a breaking free from the mistakes of the past in order to face a future that was clean and new. They were getting a second chance, and Clint didn't intend to waste one second of it.

After they'd repeated the rest of the vows, he gripped her hands and let the emotion of doing so pour over him in a flood. And it was okay. No more shoving them behind a wall and hoping they'd stay there. He wasn't his father. He knew how to control those unhealthy feelings, while giving himself over to the ones that made two people into one.

"You may kiss the bride."

"Gladly." He wrapped his arms around Jessi's waist and reeled her in. "Love you," he whispered against her lips.

"Love you, too," she mouthed back.

Only then did he allow himself to really kiss her, putting his heart and soul into the joining of their lips.

"Whooo…" The sound came from the seats behind them, growing in volume the longer the kiss went on.

Clint smiled and leaned back, allowing his hands to slide down her arms until he was clasping her fingers once again. His grandmother's small diamond glittered up at him, a promise of the future. A promise further evidenced by the ultrasound in a drawer in his office desk. Jessi was expecting. A surprise to both of them. And for someone who'd thought he'd never be a father, it was another emotional first. A good one, though.

Jessi squeezed his hands and then turned to motion Chelsea and her new fiancé up to the front.

Paul had proposed just a week ago, and Chelsea had accepted, so there would be more wedding bells in the future. And probably more births along this crazy path they were all on. Her daughter hugged her long and hard, while Paul shook Clint's hand and wished him well.

Then Clint wrapped his arm around his new bride, while the minister introduced them as Mr. Clint and Mrs. Jessica Marks.

Smiles and cheers from some army buddies and their families and friends came from all around them.

This was where he belonged. He'd faced his deepest fears and they hadn't destroyed him. They'd given him hope.

Hope for a future filled with happiness as well as trials, but, most important, love.

"Shall we?"

Jessi grasped his hand and ran down the aisle, half dragging him along with her.

"What's the rush, Mrs. Marks," he asked.

They reached the door and pushed through it. "I've been waiting all morning for the chance to smash a piece of wedding cake all over your face."

"That's more exciting to you than us getting married?"

"No." She threw him a happy grin. "It's what comes after that has me all worked up."

"Dare I ask what that is?"

"You could, but you might not want me to explain in a public venue."

He laughed, his heart lighter than the frothy layers of his bride's cream-colored dress that fluttered around her knees.

"Then lead on, woman. We've got a cake to cut."

* * * * *

Look out for Tina Beckett's next Medical Romance™
HER PLAYBOY'S SECRET
Available in July 2015
Don't miss this final installment of the
fabulous MIDWIVES ON-CALL *series!*

MILLS & BOON®
Hardback – April 2015

ROMANCE

MILLS & BOON®
Large Print – April 2015

ROMANCE

Taken Over by the Billionaire	Miranda Lee
Christmas in Da Conti's Bed	Sharon Kendrick
His for Revenge	Caitlin Crews
A Rule Worth Breaking	Maggie Cox
What The Greek Wants Most	Maya Blake
The Magnate's Manifesto	Jennifer Hayward
To Claim His Heir by Christmas	Victoria Parker
Snowbound Surprise for the Billionaire	Michelle Douglas
Christmas Where They Belong	Marion Lennox
Meet Me Under the Mistletoe	Cara Colter
A Diamond in Her Stocking	Kandy Shepherd

HISTORICAL

Strangers at the Altar	Marguerite Kaye
Captured Countess	Ann Lethbridge
The Marquis's Awakening	Elizabeth Beacon
Innocent's Champion	Meriel Fuller
A Captain and a Rogue	Liz Tyner

MEDICAL

It Started with No Strings...	Kate Hardy
One More Night with Her Desert Prince...	Jennifer Taylor
Flirting with Dr Off-Limits	Robin Gianna
From Fling to Forever	Avril Tremayne
Dare She Date Again?	Amy Ruttan
The Surgeon's Christmas Wish	Annie O'Neil

MILLS & BOON®
Hardback – May 2015

ROMANCE

MILLS & BOON®
Large Print – May 2015

ROMANCE

The Secret His Mistress Carried	Lynne Graham
Nine Months to Redeem Him	Jennie Lucas
Fonseca's Fury	Abby Green
The Russian's Ultimatum	Michelle Smart
To Sin with the Tycoon	Cathy Williams
The Last Heir of Monterrato	Andie Brock
Inherited by Her Enemy	Sara Craven
Taming the French Tycoon	Rebecca Winters
His Very Convenient Bride	Sophie Pembroke
The Heir's Unexpected Return	Jackie Braun
The Prince She Never Forgot	Scarlet Wilson

HISTORICAL

Marriage Made in Money	Sophia James
Chosen by the Lieutenant	Anne Herries
Playing the Rake's Game	Bronwyn Scott
Caught in Scandal's Storm	Helen Dickson
Bride for a Knight	Margaret Moore

MEDICAL

Playing the Playboy's Sweetheart	Carol Marinelli
Unwrapping Her Italian Doc	Carol Marinelli
A Doctor by Day...	Emily Forbes
Tamed by the Renegade	Emily Forbes
A Little Christmas Magic	Alison Roberts
Christmas with the Maverick Millionaire	Scarlet Wilson

MILLS & BOON®

Why shop at millsandboon.co.uk?

Each year, thousands of romance readers find their perfect read at millsandboon.co.uk. That's because we're passionate about bringing you the very best romantic fiction. Here are some of the advantages of shopping at www.millsandboon.co.uk:

* **Get new books first**—you'll be able to buy your favourite books one month before they hit the shops

* **Get exclusive discounts**—you'll also be able to buy our specially created monthly collections, with up to 50% off the RRP

* **Find your favourite authors**—latest news, interviews and new releases for all your favourite authors and series on our website, plus ideas for what to try next

* **Join in**—once you've bought your favourite books, don't forget to register with us to rate, review and join in the discussions

Visit **www.millsandboon.co.uk**
for all this and more today!